BADGER'S
LEGACY

BADGER'S LEGACY

Warrior

Joseph Malcolm Leonard

iUniverse, Inc.
Bloomington

BADGER'S LEGACY
WARRIOR

iUniverse books may be ordered through booksellers or by contacting:

iUniverse
1663 Liberty Drive
Bloomington, IN 47403
www.iuniverse.com
1-800-Authors (1-800-288-4677)

ISBN: 978-1-4620-5077-2 (sc)
ISBN: 978-1-4620-5078-9 (ebk)

Printed in the United States of America

iUniverse rev. date: 09/12/2011

1

Remembrance

The planet of Statureo is about twice the size of earth. It has one sun, and is orbited by two moons which by size are not very interesting. They are simply two rock balls Staturians can see. They are on completely opposite sides so day or night one is always visible. Statureo has two continents about equal to Asia then a third about the size of South America. There is a wide range of land features such as mountains, sprawling plains with patches of exotic multicolored flowers, forests with shades of green mixed with occasional orange, desert, plus rivers of all sizes especially the snake which flows along the edge of a swamp called the Okoba. The planet with it's abundance of food supplies hundreds if not thousands of species of birds, reptiles, and mammals. Also developed are some life which are close in nature to what you would find on earth. On the night Miranda was forced to choose a place for escape the orange eye picked a world that had some similarities. Because of this that is how earth became a small battlefield in the war. This chance of fate is what Badger owes for first meeting Miranda. A very beautiful night had developed after a cloudy day. Watching from his vantage point amongst the cliffs Badger looks out over the town of Liberty. There were so many things that had happened since his arrival to this place. Many good friends had been lost in the struggle. A cool breeze blew as numerous stars sparkled in the night sky.

Badger had been riding in Liberty earlier in the day. He still found himself asking if the fighting could have been avoided. In reality there were no other options. Those with the reigns of power had to be stopped. The town of Liberty did not exist before his arrival. Liberty is the capitol of the Covehi who can be a fierce enemy when they are pushed into a corner. This has been Badger's home for quite some time now. During that time he has not regretted his decisions.

Stopping the Mordagi was no easy task. They were a strong force to contend with. Badger came from a different land to fight the evil that threatened this world. The circumstances that led up to the traveling is a amazing tell. Where he did come from was no utopia. Mankind was on it's way to self destruction. Chaos was becoming the norm for society. You would also find Badger giving the local fire district a hand. Don't get it wrong. Good people were still around but their numbers were dropping at an alarming rate. Badger witnessed officers gunned down without a chance. Things like that made him decide to go with Miranda, and fight the evil in her world.

After fifty years Badger has begun to feel his age. Soon his son will take over the presidency. Miranda has been gone now for two years. It already feels like an eternity to him. How he misses her smile, laughter, and joy they had together. What they shared was indeed special. The Liber river is where Badger first met Torman. The key organizer of the resistance. They had been friends ever since.

Badger's thoughts are disturbed when he hears someone walking down the trail. Turning he sees Torman.

"I was right. I figured you were up here. O'zar is back."

"Good. I am feeling old my friend."

"No one lives forever. You have seen many things. War replaced with peace. O'zar about to take the presidency. Not bad my friend."

"Thank you Torman. Who would have ever thought a guy like me from Illinois would have such a wild life."

"You know Badger. In all these years you have not talked much about where you came from."

"There were several reasons I made the plunge. My homeland seemed like a lost cause. Felt I could make a difference here. Finally, I have to admit I was greatly smitten by Miranda. Who would have thought she would become my wife."

Torman cannot resist a chuckle as he leans up against a tree. Badger continued. It was a quiet evening as he read a book. He had started to eat a roast beef sandwich when he was interrupted by a serious message from a radio on a coffee table. Except for Oakridge all of the county got fire protection from volunteers.

"Attention all Hickory Valley personnel you have a structure fire at 3800 north 370 east."

Because of his position as a deputy sheriff he was able to drive his cruiser to the fire station. Within five minutes he was there helping crew an engine. Badger found himself responding with Duke Mulligan. As they were responding additional crews had also gone in rout plus a Burke county deputy had arrived to inform them it was a fully involved house.

"Sounds like we are going to be busy."

"Sure does Duke."

When they arrive the two find themselves donning air packs, and going straight to work. The deputy chief had already set up help from Oakridge, Springhill, and Crystal Creek fire districts. After a few hours the job got done. Thankfully it is found out the owners are out of town.

The next day Jeff Bullock comes by to visit Badger.

"Hey there Dan. Sounded like quite a night."

"You could say that. What are you up to?"

"Wanted to see if you wanted to have dinner with us tonight. Rachel is cooking up something good."

"Not tonight. Plus I still remember what you tried last time."

"Hey, I really thought you two would hit it off."

At this point his friend had finally provoked a hostile response.

"Listen real good! I want no more talk about my solitary life."

Badger sees his friend taken aback.

"Ok buddy. I have to go. Catch you later."

As Badger watches his friend drive away he thinks about his friend's good intentions. The only thing was Badger was a special case. He thinks some people are just destined to be loners.

2

Night Visitors

"Four Paul 33"

Badger promptly answered.

"Four Paul 33 check reports of possible trespassers on Charlie Kingdales property off of Coal Creek drive. That should be close to 3680 north 400 east. Mr. Kingdale is the caller advising he saw several lights flashing in the woods to the east of his cornfield. He's requesting area be checked."

Upon his arrival he quickly turned off the headlights. Badger quietly pulls to the side of the gravel road as he tells his dispatcher he will be out of the car. After exiting his vehicle Badger stands next to it for a few minutes just observing the woods for movement. There was still nothing after five minutes. Grabbing his flashlight he begins to walk into the cornfield. Also about midway through a artfully constructed scarecrow had been placed with evidence the cornfield had just recently been plowed. It was at that point that Badger saw a red light flash just inside the woods. Kneeling down next to the scarecrow he observes several more flashes within minutes of each other. The caterwauling of horses, and men can be heard as shadows begin to move in the tree line. Badger decides to call for additional help on the radio.

"Four Paul 33 to dispatch"

"Go ahead Paul 33"

"Respond me assistance. I do have several subjects in the woods. Unknown what the exact situation is. Some appear to be on horseback."

"Ten four Paul 33. Attention all units 33 needing assistance off of Coal Creek drive. He has several trespassers. Units responding advise."

"Four Paul 22 responding"

"Four Paul 23 responding from Bakersville"

"Four Paul 25 on the way"

"Four Paul 28 responding"

"Four Paul 29 also dispatch"

"Four Paul 35 reponding out of Oakridge"

During his call for backup three figures had emerged from the woods. They were all on horses. The men appeared to be armed with what looked like crossbows. It was hard to tell in the darkness. There was only limited moonlight.

As he reached to take out his sidearm from it's holster one of the riders pointed out towards his car. Badger decided to have dispatch see if the state had any troopers in the area that could respond also. At that time he could make out red lights coming from a cruiser in the distance. The riders evidently saw it also. Immediately they became agitated. They had closed the distance between them. At this point there was no mistaking their weaponry. They were crossbows, and very impressive swords. With weapon drawn Badger stands making his presence known.

"Deputy Sheriff stay right where you are"

All three riders sat in their mounts just looking at him. Badger informed them to dismount, and that they were under arrest. By now sirens could be heard. There was still a lot of activity in the woods. Out of the corner of his eye he caught a movement. A person was preparing to fire a crossbow at him. With reflexes like a steel trap Badger turned placing two well placed shots into the assailants chest. Two of the riders began to retreat, while the third rushed him. Badger taking aim, fired, and made sure it was the last thing the charging rider ever saw.

A deputy pulled his squad car behind Badger's. Others were right behind him. Badger bent down to make sure he had a full round of ammunition. Another red light began to glow in the woods. Several figures were scrambling for it.

By now several deputies and state troopers had arrived with more still coming. They had begun to cross the field.

Continuing to scan the woods intensely Badger waits for additional officers to catch up to him. Within minutes a skirmish line is established. Each man leaving about five feet between each other. Men, and horses alike continued for the light.

They took no more than a few steps when a band of five riders charged them from the woods. They were preparing to fire with their crossbows. Officers stood in their tracks, and opened fire. A few deputies had their shotguns with them. In minutes five riders hit the ground the hard way. Although they were able to stop them one was able to hit his mark. Trooper Cumbers received the fatal shot. It was probably the most amazing or just luckiest shot ever. Right through the head. He was dead before touching the ground. During this confrontation the red glow had disappeared. After several hours of intensive searching nothing was found. All they had were seven suspects who were not going to be able to tell them anything. There were not even any clues to who they were. What they were doing. Badger considers how it would have been nice if this would have happened on his night off instead.

"I don't get it Lewiston. There was something going on in there. How could men, and horses just vanish like that?'"

"Beyond me Dan. Seventeen years with this department, and never has anything so bizarre ever even remotely happened during that time. One thing is for certain though. We had better be watching our backs. Hopefully the investigators can come up with something."

When Badger gets home that night he notices a piece of glass resembling a diamond in the back seat of his police cruiser. The fact that it was orange in color had caught his eye. Badger carried it into the kitchen gently placing it on a wooden table. He decided to wait till the next day to try to figure out what it was thus what to do with it. He settles down to get a quick news broadcast to see what has been happening. "Good evening, the United States has pledged full support to the Kuwaiti government after proof the Iranian military has begun a extensive buildup of military assets that could prove a threat to the small Arab country.

Also in the region an Iranian fighter was shot down today when it approached too closely to the U.S.S. Ronald Reagan: a carrier assigned to the area. The U.S. says warnings were given but ignored. Iran responded by promising to avenge the shoot down in a most equitable manner.

The defense department announced a successful test of the missile defense system known as protector.

Meanwhile in Chicago police say gangs were responsible for the shooting death of a judge. No arrests have been made."

Nothing seemed to get better. At around four in the morning the rock began to glow. It ended abruptly not disturbing Badger's slumber. Badger had put in a lot of overtime early in the month so he decided to take a couple days off. The contract allowed him to as long as they had the time which was no problem for him.

During that time Badger decided to visit Mark Roman one evening. Mark was in his early twenties, brown hair, 5'5, and somewhat stocky. Like usual when he got there Mark was doing something on the computer. It was a hobby he would always say. Mark owned a real nice house. He could afford it though; he was a top executive at a factory in Oakridge. Oakridge was a fair sized city in Burke County. Mark even had a billiards table. That's where they moved to. The two friends had always felt it was a relaxing activity. After a sorely missed shot by Mark he could not resist a friendly verbal taunt.

"Maybe I should go get you some glasses. Better yet maybe if I made the pockets bigger you might actually have a chance. What do you think?"

"I will give you some pockets to play with mister comedian."

"No thanks."

After playing for about an hour and a half there was a door bell ring. Mark went to answer it, and returned in the company of Jeff Bullock.

"How are things going Dan. Has Mark managed to improve or is he still hopeless?"

"Well let me put it this way. If hell ever freezes over he might have a shot at the championship."

"Thumbs up Mark. Did I hear you are actually taking a couple of days off Dan?"

"As a matter of fact yes."

"Listen to this for a minute. I have someone you just have to meet. Single and a certified goddess. I happened to talk about you to her. She really wants a chance to meet you. What are you doing tomorrow night buddy."

"Correct me if I'm wrong but we had this discussion not to long ago."

"Sort of. I know deep down you really did not mean it. I think you are going to be impressed. I mean come on what are friends for."

Before Badger could answer Mark chimed in his agreement on the matter. Woefully outnumbered by his allies he decided to surrender.

Elsewhere plans were being made to reclaim the orange eye between Hob the wizard, and one of his generals.

"Listen well general Bishop. Send some men back for the orange eye before the rebels gain control of it. It limits my powers. I will not be able to track them. It could cause us to become vulnerable. Even now I must use other means to locate where they gather to plan resistance."

"As you command it will be done."

3

Meeting Miranda

The following evening is the first time Badger actually meets Miranda. Badger had to admit his friend had done a impressive job. She was indeed beautiful. Black hair flowing just inches below her shoulder blades. Her blue eyes were so lovely, and compelling. There was no hurry to look away. Through Jeff the arrangement was that she would meet him at his place then they would determine the rest of the night from there. She was wearing a breathtaking red dress along with high heels.

On his part he had decided to wear a dark blue suit. Once he saw her he was glad he did.

"Please come in. I hope this was not to hard to find? I know it is a little secluded out here."

"It was not to difficult. The police car helps narrow it down quite a bit."

For the first time in a long time Badger started to actually enjoy a woman's company. A sense of humor was a plus in his book.

"I guess that did help cut down on the guess work. Being a bachelor I am not usually supplied well, but I do have tea or pop if you would like something to drink?"

"I am not real thirsty right now. A little later probably. Your friend Jeff said you are a deputy. How long have you done that?"

"Almost two years now. I have an idea. There is a nice restaurant with a great dance floor in Oakridge. The only catch is that I only know how to slow dance. Tempted?"

"I think that would be very enjoyable."

As they stepped out to his mustang Badger noticed there were no other cars in sight except the squad.

"Miranda, how did you get here?"

"I had a friend bring me out here."

After a delicious meal, and exuberant slow dancing for a couple of hours Miranda wanted to know if Badger would like to retire back to his place. Since the night was going so well there were no objections from him.

Up to this point through small talk Badger felt he was making some progress on getting a better idea of who she was. For example she was new to the area, her family was out east, she worked in an office as a secretary.

Upon reaching their destination they started to get settled down in the living room.

"This has been such a relaxing night. I remember seeing something in the paper about a police officer getting killed a few days ago. Were you out in the midst of all that?"

"Actually I was. A state trooper named Cumbers died."

"The paper did not say much about what happened. How did the trooper get killed?"

"The whole incident is still under investigation. Do you have a special interest of some kind or just curiosity?"

"Attention all Hickory Valley fire personnel we have a report a power pole has been hit on route 20 close to Bakers road. Vehicle involved has three patients for medical. Deputies responding"

"Look Miranda, I should probably answer this."

"Go ahead. I will be here when you get back if that is okay."

"See you then. Bye."

It took a couple of hours for all the mess to be cleaned up but it did. The patients all got to the hospital, and were expected to be alright. All the paperwork got wrote up, and it was time to go home. On his way home Badger started to wonder more about why

11

Miranda was so interested about the night the officer got killed. Even though he had nothing to support it he had a gut feeling something was amiss.

As Badger pulled into his drive he noticed his front door partially open. Quickly turning off the engine, and headlights he slowly opens the car door. He stands for a moment to let his eyes adjust to the dark. For a night that started out so well it was taking a very odd turn. Everything seemed to be pitch black. Badger started to pick up his radio from the squad but stopped himself. Miranda may have just fallen asleep, and not meaning to left the door open. There was one precaution Badger was taking with him though. Better known as a shotgun. Badger stealthily approaches the front door. He quickly ascertains there is nobody in the living room. He enters tensed up for anything. After doing so he hears something drop to the floor. The noise originates from the bedroom. He begins to see a figure approach the doorway. He decides to lower his weapon, and places it behind a chair. With clenched fists Badger prepares for one whale of a tackle when the intruder comes through the doorway. Just as the intruder starts to make out Badger's form from the shadows Badger plows into him full force sprawling him into the floor. Upon this collision a knife goes careening down the hard wood floor. The intruder makes a grab for it but finds his arm being pulled back. Badger makes a quick connection between his opponent's jaw, and his left fist. As the unwelcome visitor goes reeling back he places a kick between Badger's legs. Badger manages to roll into the living room.

When he gets up a warning is shouted to him.

"We will do what we have to for the Orange eye to fall into our hands."

"I don't know who you are but I'm going to make you my new wallpaper."

In seconds the two combatants are in a struggle all over the place. Punches flying left, and right. Chairs even being thrown in mid air. As Badger ducks a chair his adversary makes a dash out the door. Making a bee line to a box under his bed Badger obtains another one of his sidearms. He is ready for pursuit. As he goes through the door a arrow hits the frame inches from his head. He automatically dives for cover as he is narrowly missed again. Badger rolls behind a log, stands up, and proceeds to empty a clip into the direction he was fired from. After ten minutes of holding that position Badger figures the assailant has been scared off. When Badger enters the house for the second time he realizes the orange eye is gone. If the one he just tangled with did not have it then who did. There was only one other person who could have taken it. Why would Miranda want the jewel? Why did she keep asking him about that night? He had a million questions to ask her.

4

Answers & Turmoil

The following morning was the funeral service for trooper Cumbers. There were police officers present from all over the state. Trooper Cumbers had earned respect among his colleagues through hard work, and dedication to the job. Before the service that morning Badger had decided he was going to find out who, and what Miranda wanted.

Immediately following the service Badger went to the station house. He made his way to the locker room where inside he kept a black box. As he opened it he thought about how surprised Miranda would be when she realized she had a fake. The real jewel was safely in the box. Badger had changed them around the night before he met Miranda. Seeing it was still safe he placed it back for safe keeping. Badger decided his first step to solve the mystery was to go see Jeff. When he got to Jeff's house he was out back drinking some lemonade.

"What are you doing this fine day?"

"Not a whole lot. I wanted to talk to you about Miranda?"

"Oh yeah. I have been wanting to hear how it went. Talk to me."

"It went ok. Tell me something. How did you meet her anyway?"

"I came across her walking along the road one evening. Figured maybe she could use some help. She said her car was broke down. She asked me to drive her into Oakridge. So I did. She said she was new to the area, and during our conversation I mentioned you. You know the rest. So tell me if your going to see each other again?"

"I have a feeling we will soon. I'll talk to you later."

"Hold it! Before you go I need to ask you something. Me, and Rachel decided to get married in three weeks. I'm expecting you to be my best man. How about it?"

Badger just looked at him for a minute. All of a sudden he had to let loose the smile he was holding back.

"I would be honored. I'm really happy for you."

"Thanks Dan."

Upon arriving home that evening Badger found a note attached to his door. THIS IS VERY IMPORTANT DAN. ONLY YOU KNOW WHERE THE REAL ORANGE EYE IS. I KNOW YOU KNOW I LIED TO YOU. THERE IS NO WAY YOU WOULD BELIEVE THE TRUTH. IF YOU DO NOT LET ME HAVE IT INNOCENT LIVES WILL BE LOST. I WILL BE IN CONTACT WITH YOU SOON. MIRANDA

This was becoming more intriguing as time passed.

Back in Miranda's world a discussion was underway between the wizard, and General Bishop.

"How could you fail?"

"We underestimated him."

"No! You underestimated him. Perhaps you do not deserve the rank you enjoy."

"It will not happen again. I promise you that much."

"It had better not General. I will not tolerate incompetence amongst my command. Understood?"

A very chagrined Bishop exits the room.

On earth things are proving a bit more calmer for Badger. There was a stream that flowed not very far from his residence. On a quiet evening Badger was enjoying the serenity of that stream when he saw Miranda again as he sat on a rock along the bank. Due to past events Badger was always armed now with a sidearm. Badger was wearing a dark reddish short sleeve shirt since the evenings were still warm. He was facing the stream when he hears a tree branch snap behind him. In a fluid motion he turns placing his right hand on his weapon. Miranda walks into his view. Badger seems to let his hand relax. He again realizes how breath taking she is. Her black hair was made into a pony tail, a one piece tunic made from deerskin, leather boots, two bracelets, armed with a crossbow over her shoulder, and a knife strapped to her left upper leg. Her shoulder blades, arms, and legs very visible.

"So we meet again Dan. Where is the orange eye?"

"Not until I have some answers. Like who you really are. What the hell is this orange eye thing?"

"Miranda is my real name. You would not believe the rest."

"Tell me anyway. I also want to know who I've been fighting?"

"You have been fighting the Mordagi. They come from a different place like me. We are in the middle of a war. The orange eye will play an important part in this conflict. If the royal family along with their henchmen such as the wizard gain control of it everyone will eventually become their slaves."

"You've lied to me once how do I know you are telling the truth now? I think maybe I will hold onto it for the time being until I decide what is best."

"The longer you have it the longer your life is at risk."

"Don't worry about me. I'll take care of my end."

"Please Dan. Let me have it now."

"No! Three weeks. You will have my decision then."

"So be it. Three weeks."

Miranda briskly walks into the woods to disappear from sight. During those three weeks the world continued to tear itself apart. Violence was replacing negotiation in the world's arena. Criminals were running rampant. In the bigger cities National Guard units had been called in several times to assist police in quelling large scale disturbances. The incredible arrest rates continued up for everybody. The Mordagi waited until the third week to make a move.

Badger was working Burke county again. He was driving down route 19. It was nine in the evening. Traffic was scarce that time of night in that area of the county. He was surprised when his headlights picked out somebody lying in the road. As he gets closer he is able to determine it was a woman. She had on jeans, torn blue shirt, and tennis shoes.

Once he pulls up to her, Badger turns on the reds, and notifies his dispatcher what was going on. At that time he saw no reason for additional support. When he shuts the car door, he slides his baton down it's holder. Badger then gingerly approaches the woman.

"Miss, can you hear me?"

She slowly turns to face Badger.

"I am here to help you. Are you hurt?"

Still no answer. Her eyes just staring at him. Then it happened. All four tires were hit simultaneously with arrows. Hidden behind a broken down rustic looking barn a dozen riders appeared. From the left ditch five additional men show themselves. Badger draws his sidearm to protect the woman when without warning she kicks it from his hand. He quickly thrusts his elbow back knocking her off balance. At that point Badger is charged from both sides. Badger rolls over to his weapon coming up on one knee in one quick motion. He permanently stops two coming from the left before the woman lunges at him. Badger drops to the ground so she will land on the other side of him. Quickly utilizing his handcuffs the woman finds herself shackled to the right view mirror.

A rider sprawls Badger to the ground. As he lifts his head it becomes apparent resistance has become useless. One of them starts to talk to him.

"You are a very hard man to contend with. Where is the orange eye?"

"What orange eye are you referring to?"

"We are not here to play games. If we have to we will take you with us. One last time. Where is it!"

A plan starts to form in Badger's mind. It would be a long shot but it was better then nothing.

"Okay. Let me get up."

"Leave the weapon on the ground. Then release Laroa from the binders."

If he could get the shotgun, and use Laroa as a shield that would give him time to call in reinforcements. They could not kill him outright or no orange eye so a standoff was to his advantage. Badger pulls the keys from his pocket. Instead of getting the handcuff key however he gets the key to the gun rack in the front. Badger then steps between Laroa, and the car door. The Mordagi sensing victory relax a bit. In a blur of motion Badger opens the door, throws the key into the lock, and manages to jerk out the shotgun. Two men jump on the hood ready to kick in the windshield. Badger discharges twice through the windshield which puts a end to them. He gets out standing next to Laroa.

"All of you pull back! Now none of you want Laroa to get hurt now do you?"

"Go ahead. You are alone."

"Not for long. Pull back!"

The Mordagi commander signals his men to fall back. They obey. Using his left hand Badger leans in, and grabs the radio mike.

"All I have to do is say one word, and we will have a repeat of what happened in the cornfield. A pointless firefight. You can't force an armed man to do something he does not want to do. I will release Laroa after you have gone."

"Enough! You have won this confrontation. You will not be so lucky next time."

The Mordagi commander pulls back the reigns, and turns. A portal appears. Men and horses enter to vanish from sight.

"Okay Laroa. One thing before you go. Let the wizard know I am on guard, and will not be tricked so easily again."

She is uncuffed. She just stands there for a minute. Abruptly the portal reappears, and she like the others vanish. Badger then sits back in his car while he reassures himself he was not dreaming. He finally decides to call dispatch to send him some assistance. The only thoughts being entertained in his mind is how he is going to explain this one.

Because of the times the city of Oakridge was bolstering it's police force with officers from other agencies. They even had a name for this program. It was called the dual authority enhancement system or DAES for short. Officers worked this outside their normal shifts, and the city only had to reimburse the proper agencies. It was a way to make some extra pay for those who wanted it.

The next day Badger was riding shotgun for an Oakridge police officer under this deal. His name was Shawn Raker. They had worked together in the past. At noon they broke for lunch. There was a restaurant called JOE'S CAFE they had decided to eat at.

"I'll go ahead, and get it. Be back in a minute Dan."

"Okay. I'll keep in ear on the radio."

Five minutes had not even passed when Badger heard automatic gunfire. Before getting out he got the call out for help.

"All units clear for emergency. This is Adam 17 requesting backup at 1312 Orchard Joe's Cafe for shots fired. Officers need help."

Shotgun in hand Badger quietly makes his way up to the front of the establishment. As he goes into the front door prepared to fire at the slightest movement he sees Raker face down on the floor. Several patrons were laying face down also. A visual check confirmed the responsible person or persons had already fled out the back. Looking down Badger could see that Raker did not even have a chance to pull his weapon. At that point customers began getting up. Sirens had begun to sound outside.

To the average person it must have been quite a light show. Police cars representing Oakridge, Sheriff's dept., and state police were present not to mention the ambulance, and rescue. It almost seemed like crime was becoming unstoppable. They were the front line troops. They were losing bad. A new addition was made to the list of fallen heroes. The next several hours are taken up by the investigators asking questions about the incident. Badger makes it home that evening exhausted. The next day Jeff called.

"Hello."

"Dan. It's me Jeff. I heard about the shooting. You doing okay?"

"I guess so. I'm taking the week off. We're losing control of everything. Nothing is in order."

"Hang in there. Things will get better you'll see."

"I hope you are right Jeff."

"That's the spirit. I called to make sure you are still up for the wedding. I would hate to lose my best man."

"You bet."

"Great. Talk to you later."

The next three nights Badger is disturbed by dreams of destruction. The first night he has visions of men on horseback destroying villages. Mercy shown to nobody. He awakes in a pool of sweat. It was midnight.

The second night he sees a vision of the wizard with a group of his generals. There beings were so evil it sent chills down his spine. He awakes at midnight in a pool of sweat.

The third night he kept replaying the shooting of Raker trying to see if there was something he should have done different. He could hear Miranda's soft voice telling him there was nothing he could have done. At midnight he awakes again in a pool of sweat. Badger had also made a decision that would change his life forever. Before carrying it out though he had some important matters to take care of.

5

Decision

The next day was Jeff's wedding. Following the wedding Badger gives them his deepest congratulations. As they drive off he knows he will most likely never see them again. After a quick change of clothes it was time to take a drive over to the station. After opening his locker Badger stuffs the orange eye into a bag he had brought with him. Midnight was a ways off so Badger decided to leave a note explaining his disappearance along with a final goodbye to his friends.

When midnight arrived he was at the stream. Miranda was standing by the water.

"Did you bring the orange eye?"

"Yes. Along with that I am going with you."

"What? Why? There is no reason for you to go with me."

"You do not get the orange eye unless I go with you. My world is lost. There is a chance I can help make a difference in your world."

"Is it truly what you want Dan?"

"Yes Miranda."

"You must understand I may not be able to bring you back."

"I accept the risk."

"Than let us begin."

She places her hands in the air. A red circular shape begins to take form. It quickly solidifies into a perfect circle. A sudden movement in some bushes catches Badger's eye. Before going to meet Miranda he had put on a long coat. Badger had done this for a reason. Two Dobermans with red piercing eyes breaking from concealment were blocking their path. Badger removes the coat to reveal a arsenal. Miranda just gives a shocked grin. Badger's gun belt, and shoulder holster both have sidearms. In addition four ammunition holders completely full of ammo, two pairs of cuffs, several throwing stars, a fully loaded shotgun carried by a strap on the left shoulder, camouflage pants with pockets full of ammo for the shotgun, a knife strapped to the lower right leg, and three grenades stolen from the secret police armory. At this point it was obvious the dogs were set to attack. There was no time to lose. Simultaneously as his right hand goes for the sidearm, and his left hand goes for the shoulder they launch themselves in midair towards the pair. Badger is able to inflict fatal shots to both Dobermans before they can reach their targets. Each from a different gun.

"We must hurry. Once we get to my world I can keep the wizard from tracking us."

"I'm all set."

They both enter the portal without hesitation. Once through it rapidly closes behind them. The only evidence they had been there were two Dobermans that in their death seemed to transform into creatures not natural to our world. Of course this knowledge Badger will not know since he is already on the other side of the portal. In a second Badger finds himself on another world. He was becoming more intrigued by Miranda. Somehow he felt she was gaining a fondness for him. They found themselves in a forested area.

"Now that we are here where are the resistance fighters?"

"They are about two days travel from here. The leaders name is Torman."

They begin their trek which slows because of a thickening of the forest.

"Why did you truly come Dan?"

"Because I want to help."

"You are not that simple of a man. There must be more to it. Why won't you tell me?"

"Maybe I am not completely sure why myself. Just that I need to."

"I find you to be a very interesting man. How was it you had no wife? That surprises me."

At first Badger thought they would meet up with Torman without incident. Like usual he was wrong. Unknown to him a band of Mordagi were approaching from the opposite direction. A collision course. They of course did not know that. Miranda was able to sense their approach. The band consisted of eleven riders. They were riding three abreast with one in front, and one hanging back behind the main body. All armed with the usual crossbows. To go around them would have cost valuable time. Badger decides it is time to let the Mordagi know he is still around. The path was lined with hills on both sides. Even better was that the area was still forested. His decision is to ambush them. He carefully positions himself to get the best field of fire he can. Miranda goes to the opposite side of him to sit it out on his insistence. Once in position the wait is not very long.

Badger waits for the main body to just get in front of him. He takes careful aim, and opens fire. Two of the riders in the middle go down. At that point the riders in the rear pull their crossbows while the front five begin to spread out looking for his position. Two more go down before they spot him. The three in the front break into two groups. One starts to ride out to raise the alarm. The other two start up the hill. One rider begins a direct line to Badger. The remaining riders wait as they try to line up their shots. Badger nails the one going for help then throws a star at the one charging him. A perfect throw into the upper chest. He quickly rolls to some different trees. From these trees he starts using the shotgun. After four shots three more of the enemy are eliminated from this new battlefield. Badger goes behind another tree, and decides to climb it. The remaining two dismount, and make their final approach on foot. As they pass under him he drops down just behind them. Two quick shots finish the job. The Mordagi were spread along the path, and hillside alike. In Badger's first encounter on Statureo a Mordagi patrol has been destroyed. An eleven band Mordagi patrol was destroyed. Badger walks down the path to join Miranda who is waiting for him. She softly puts her hand on his shoulder. They both lock gazes. They both feel something but neither are willing to admit it. Badger is the one to break the silence.

"We should probably not linger. It's only a matter of time before more of their buddies happen by. They will not be very happy."

"Whatever you say."

Once mounted they begin their last leg of their journey to meet Torman.

"This is beautiful land. The streams, big trees, and a breathtaking sky. Hard to believe there is a war on."

"There is not much of the land without scars anymore. This is one of the few areas."

"Were you born with your powers? Are there others like you Miranda or are you a special case?"

"There was a time when I was part of a sisterhood. The sisterhood was peaceful. That was before the wizard called us a threat. A danger to his control. He sent his forces to the wetlands where we resided. Only a handful escaped the attack. Out of that most were taken prisoner. There is only one other still opposing the wizard. Her name is Kanessa. She fights alone. It is not known for sure where she is."

"Doesn't she trust anybody?"

"No."

"Your powers connected could be a valuable weapon."

"Wait. Torman is very close. We are being watched by one of his scouts."

"Where is the scout at?"

"I would not be asking that question if I were you whoever you are. I am Torman. Leader of the rebels."

Badger turns to his left, and out from some trees five riders emerge. In the middle is Torman. All wearing about the same. Buckskin, using crossbows with swords as weaponry. The only difference at first glance is that Torman is riding a black mount while the others are brown. Torman is in his late twenties, and sports a moustache.

"It is good to see you back Miranda. You bring back a stranger with you this time. Who is it?"

"This is Dan Badgerman. He comes from where I traveled to. He is a good man. He has come to help in the fight against the wizard."

"Why did you come here Badgerman? This is not your fight. Chances are you will never leave here."

"I know the risk. I am here for reasons only I can understand."

"You sound like a philosopher not a fighter. Sure you can fight?"

Miranda's voice rings out.

"He can fight. There is a band of eleven Mordagi who can no longer be a threat to us due to his skills."

"Well, looks can be deceiving. Forgive me for my hasty judgement. If Miranda says you are a fighter than you are a fighter. Welcome to our clan. Come, there is a meeting at camp tonight."

"Thank you Torman."

"Oh. One last question. What are those objects you carry with you?"

"I call them pieces of peace."

"How powerful are they?"

"Let me demonstrate. See that squirrel on the other side of the stream."

"Yes."

Badger draws a sidearm, takes aim, and fires just below it's feet. It jumps running the fastest probably witnessed before for such a small creature. Badger holsters his weapon without a word. Torman stares, and after a minute breaks into laughter.

"You are a man full of surprises my friend."

A short fifteen minutes later they ride into camp. Torman stops, and begins talking to a guard.

"Kalip my friend. How goes the homefront?"

"Could always be better Torman. Scouts have reported Mordagi in places they normally are not in. We sent out two patrols within the last couple of days. Have not seen them since. Lot of people getting worried."

"I understand. Things are not exactly in our favor. Any word from Morot?"

"Nothing yet. Do you really think the Argonnes will help us?"

"It is hard to tell. I do not even know if Morot made it to their territory. He was one of the best we could send. We should know something soon."

"Who is the stranger with you?"

"He came back with Miranda. He is a fighter. Just call him Badger."

After that comment the group begins to make their way through the camp. There were men sitting by campfires, while others were practicing sword play. Small wooden structures were built in groups of three. Each group had a fire. Horses were scattered amongst the encampment. The warriors ages ranged from seventeen to late fifties. This was the first true look Badger had of the men fighting this horrible war. Their faces were grim as they passed by. Good fighting evil in the most classical way..

They ride up to a log cabin where two men are posted.

"Dismount. Trinit, go tell the sergeants they are to be here for a war meeting tonight."

"Whatever you say Torman."

"Were you successful Miranda?"

"The orange eye is in our possesion."

At that point Badger takes the orange eye out of a pouch he had been carrying with him, and hands it to Miranda.

"Good."

Badger interjects a question to Torman.

"How powerful are your forces compared to the wizards?"

"We have a strength near three hundred. The wizard is backed by no less than a thousand Mordagi fighters. He also has swamp chameleons fighting for him."

"What the hell are swamp chameleons?"

"They are a four legged race. High intelligience from what we know. They can be quite aggresive. The wizard has evidently struck a deal with them. They are able to change their form. To fight though they must go back to their true form. The weapon they fight with is the poison orb. It is said they control the orbs with their minds. Such control they can only use in close quarters. A sting from one of the orbs is instant death. There is no antidote to their poison. They also have a hide equivalent to armor. Nothing known can penetrate it. Except for a small part of their underbelly which is soft weapons can't hurt them.

6

War Council

That night Torman holds a meeting with his command staff. Badger accompanied by Miranda are also present. His sergeants are as follows Glite, Loptoe, Twistle, Cheelo, and Zandra.

Glite has blond hair, blue eyes, slender build, 5'7, and before the war had been a guide for travelers going through the Shastle mountains. Glite controls all scouts, and camp security. Like the others except for Loptoe he was in his late twenties.

Loptoe was in his late forties, and a well respected man by all. He was known as probably the best hunter there was. Also what we would consider a judge in one of the towns that no longer exists. Loptoe saw to training decisions. He was trying hard to turn this rabble of men into a well trained force.

Twistle is a short, rowdy, high spirited man. He was 5'5, brown hair, hazel eyes, and a scar on his left arm. A knife wound he received in the midst of a disagreement at a drinking establishment before the war of course. Twistle saw to long range assignments when they came up.

Cheelo has a pretty big build. He got it from working with metals. His specialty was making swords. Cheelo was the only black fighter in the movement. There were few blacks in the entire territory. Most lived in the Hylatorian province. Torman had divided his forces in two basic structures. Mounted assault group, and ground assault group. The ground assault group consisting of those best suited for archery service. Mounted was better suited for quick strike, and close combat such as swords. Cheelo had the mounted assault group under his command.

The ground assault group was under the command of Zandra who was the only female fighter Torman had. Her hatred for the Mordagi was intense. She had lost a husband, and the whereabouts of two children unknown. She had long brown hair, blue eyes, and pleasing disposition.

"At this time I want to welcome back Miranda. She also has managed to bring back a new ally. The best news is that she has been successful."

Glite offered a praise.

"Honor to Miranda for her success will give us extra fire against the wizard."

"Sgt. Glite what are the movements of the Mordagi?"

"Large numbers have begun to approach closer to this camp then ever before. I am unable to tell if it is just their normal searching patterns or if they are working from information."

"From your latest reports how close are they?"

"Two large camps we have noticed setting up to our north and south would be a good 7 days away. I did however receive a report of a twenty man patrol coming directly towards us from the east. If not intercepted they will be here in two days."

"Sgt. Zandra."

"Yes Torman."

"Assign a ten man unit out to change their direction. Tell them to make it look like a accidental contact, and lead them out to the Olo crossroads. At that point they should head into Hykolite territory. Once they have been gone for a couple of weeks tell them to rejoin our forces. If they can't find us they should survey the length of the Liber to find us."

"Yes Torman."

"Sgt. Cheelo. Do you have any mounted troops out at this time?"

"No sir all troops in at this time."

"I am ready for strategy ideas. Keep in mind our freedom of movement is now better."

"I say we send a force of one hundred up north to strike the stronghold of Morrill. The Mordagi must know we are here. They have never been this close before. Such an attack would make them think we have moved."

"I agree with Cheelo."

"Such an attack would be very bold Twistle. Yet we could lose an awful lot for which we could not afford to lose."

"Yes Torman but if the Mordagi have found us our defenses are not strong enough anyway."

Loptoe decided it was time to enter the conversation.

"Perhaps we should consider moving or splitting into two groups if they continue to be close. The men need to continue training in so much."

As Torman pauses to think of an answer a feminine voice is heard.

"Gentleman, I have but one thing to say. At this point if either plan were adopted we would lose. I propose multiple actions. Send the attack force to Morrill, while moving camp to the southwest. A small unit should get the orange eye to the mountain caves where it will be safe. Hopefully Morot will have returned with good news by than."

"Well. My men become bolder. What is your opinion Badger?"

"I don't think the tactics you have brought up will work against the numbers of the enemy. How do you plan to get past the swamp chameleons before they give early warning of the impending attack?"

"What is your idea on fighting the wizard? Throw a few spitballs, and hope for the best."

"By no means. My plan would include many steps. The first would be to redirect that Mordagi patrol. Send Miranda with a group of your best men to locate Kanessa, and enlist her help. Form several small man units to go out, and strike at small Mordagi patrols. The time for hitting strong targets is not here yet."

As Twistle starts to respond Torman speaks up. When he wanted Torman had a way of commanding an audience.

"Here are my decisions. We will send a ten man unit to change the direction of the Mordagi. Sergeant Cheelo with an escort of twenty of our best men will take Miranda to the mountain caves with the orange eye where it will be safer. At this time this will stay our base camp. I also authorize hit, and run raids on Mordagian outposts in the north. Strategy will not deviate until further notice."

Back at the wizards fortress a meeting was under way between the wizard, and one of his generals.

"General Cymon. General Bishops incompetent handling of this interlopers affair is becoming very annoying. Since you are in charge of the hunter teams it is now your responsibility to see to his destruction."

"Yes my potentate. I have deployed ten hunter teams in the forrest of Eld. We found a patrol there. We beleive their destruction is his handiwork."

"Keep me informed."

Meanwhile even though the meeting involving Torman, and his men has ended a new discussion has begun. Two lone men stand inside.

"I want to lead your ambush force."

"Badger. That could put me at odds with my own men."

"I destroyed an eleven man Mordagi patrol using my methods, and tactics. Let me show your men how to create mayhem on the Mordagi where they are most vulnerable. Our actions will at least force them to stretch their resources. It will play hell with their planning."

After a few minutes of intense thought by Torman he gives a sigh of resignation.

"I will give you a ten man unit. Take two weeks to inflict damage on the Mordagi. Teach them all the tricks to the trade you can. If successful they can form more after you get back. We need time more than anything right now."

"Set the crew up, and I am ready to start tomorrow."

"They will be ready by afternoon. One last thing though. For now you hold authority only on those men."

"Understood. You can count on me."

7

Danger Closing

In the forest of Eld to the south of the freedom fighters encampment one of their scouts spies a hunter team. It is evening. The hunter team consists of five Mordagi, and two German shepherds. Two of the men appear to be on watch while the other three sit at a fire eating. One dog is holding a vigil over the horses while the other is eating. The scout watches from his position which is in a tree. He watches for a short span of time knowing Torman must receive notice of this situation. At this point the enemy is less then three days away. He knows what he needs to do. With great care he climbs down the tree. As he nears the base of the tree his horse starts to act jittery. All of a sudden a iron ball slams into it's neck. The horse instantly drops to the ground.

The scout is quick to the ground. A survey quickly reveals the location of a swamp chameleon. The creature is directly in front of him.

At the Mordagi camp the dogs begin to growl in the direction of the scout, and chameleon. Two of the Mordagi accompanied with one canine begin to walk in the direction of the fight.

The scout pulls his sword. The poison orb rises from it's victim. It promptly dives for the scout. Seconds before it would have hit him he dives to the ground at just the right second. As the orb misses he rolls to a perfect position to drive his sword into the underbelly of

32

the chameleon. The foul creature slumps to the ground. The victor hears a growling noise behind him. He turns in time to see sharp teeth of a canine lunging at him. The German sherpherd goes for the throat. Within seconds it is over. The startled scout is finished. News of this will not reach Torman.

A discussion is quickly held.

"It would appear the enemy is close after all."

"I must agree. It could be the group our spy has been warning us about. We need to send word to General Cymon. He will alert the other hunter teams, and move our attack forces even closer. Meanwhile we stay right here."

"I will dispatch Marst back with a dog to alert General Cymon."

"Very well."

Back at camp Sergeant Zandra was receiving last minute instructions.

"Remember your goal. Get them to change direction. Avoid outright contact. I need you all back if at all possible. Once you have changed their direction go to the east as far as the Olo crossroads. Divide into two smaller groups then filter back. Good luck!"

"No problem Torman. If we have to getting lost in the crowds of Olo should not be to hard."

A silent nod is given as they turn, and ride out.

"There they go. By the way Badger. I beleive Twistle has your band formed. Report to him so you can meet your men."

"On my way."

As Badger proceeds to meet up with Twistle his thoughts are of Miranda. Feelings had grown strong, and deep for her. As he passes a tent Miranda's voice beckons to him. He stops to see Miranda standing at the entrance.

"I hear Torman has given you control of the raiding party. When do you leave?"

"Miranda. There is something I want you to know."

"No. We will see each other soon. Be careful!"

"I love you Miranda. I'll see you soon."

Miranda just stands there. Two pairs of eyes just gazing into the others. Nothing is said. It does not have to be. Hearts have been matched. A kiss is shared amongst them. Badger's voice breaks the silence.

"I have got to go, and locate Twistle. I have decided to leave tomorrow morning. Be back later tonight."

8

Badger's Band

Badger finds Twistle near a group of mounts.

"Sgt. Twistle. Corporal Badger reporting."

"Badger. Your men are waiting to meet you. Right there just over the horizon."

"Fair enough. By the way it's corporal Badger. Don't forget again."

Before actually approaching the men he decides to observe them for a few minutes. Most are working on their swordmanship skills. Those left seemed to be working on riding skills. As a group they did not look to bad. The time for introductions was at hand. As he joins them the men quickly line up in a orderly manner. Badger walks the line.

"Illio sir."

"Jot sir."

"You can drop the sir men."

"Jolo from Juper."

"What is Juper?"

"My birth place which was destroyed by the Mordagi."

"Ribble."

"Kolabar."

"Chingat from the enslaved town of Chop."

"Crale."

"Dorad."

"Glop."

"Lucas."

"It is good to meet you all. All of you look to be in your twenties. Is that correct on my part?"

One of the band steps forward to give a firm response.

"That is correct."

"Thank you Jolo."

"The type of fighting I am going to teach you is a game of deception. To trick, and confuse the enemy. Such tactics were helpful at times where I come from. Any questions?"

"Would that not be very time consuming?"

"Good question. Right now the numbers are stacked against you immensely. You need time most of all. This kind of fighting could put them off balance. An enemy off balance has a hard time thinking, and planning. That is what you need."

Jot speaks up.

"We are not armed as you though. It is a bigger risk for us."

"This type of fighting gives the advantage to the smaller number. That you will see first hand. Now if there are no more questions we saddle up first daylight."

Darkness has begun to fall over the camp when a lone figure approaches the tent that Miranda is in. A wolf is heard howling in the distance.

The following morning Badger awakes to sounds of preparations being made for the journey. He leans over to administer a kiss to his love. Her eyes open.

"You will not wander from my thoughts. Promise me you will return safe."

"Nothing will keep me away from you Miranda. There are things for us to talk about. Plans to be made. See you in a couple of weeks."

He quickly dresses. Putting his weapons on last. Badger emerges from the tent feeling invincible. As he is putting the saddle on his mount Jot, Illio, and Chingat ride up.

"Most of the men are ready."

"Thank you Jot."

With one foot in the stirrup he mounts his black steed.

"Let us join the others."

They ride to the center of camp where all the men have assembled. A line is quickly formed. Jot, Illio, and Chingat join the ranks. Badger rides over to Torman who is present. Torman moves to the front of the row to offer final instructions.

"Corporal Badger is the commander of this unit. His orders are to harass the Mordagi in the north. He will be instructing you in ways you are to learn, and become masters at. I expect to see all of you back in three weeks. Good luck!"

Elsewhere Zandra had made visual contact with the Mordagi. The force was continuing their movement towards camp.

"Trulip."

"Yes Sgt. Zandra."

They have two scouts riding quite a ways out front. Remember where the trail goes right alongside a burned out farm. Pick two other men, and eliminate them their. After you are done make sure you leave a noticeable trail back as if you left in a hurry. That should get their attention. Such action should cause them to pursue us.

"That should not be hard to do."

"Very well. Based on their progress you should have about an hour to set up for them. Just remember Torman is counting on us."

At that Zandra along with the remainder of her band head east riding their mounts at a steady gallup.

At camp Cheelo has assembled the men who are going to safeguard Miranda to the Shastle mountain caves.

"Exactly how long are you wanting us to stay there?"

"I will send a message to you soon. I am becoming more, and more uneasy about the Mordagi getting so close. We may end up being forced to relocate camp. When Badger brought up Kanessa he had a strong point. I have much to think about."

"Whatever your decision it will be a good one. Miranda with the orange eye will remain safe. That I promise."

"Yes my friend. You have always been dependable."

"We will leave tonight. We shall use the Daga trail. It is not used much anymore."

The forest is such a quiet place as the sun begins to fall. The sound of hoofbeats are heard approaching in the distance. In a matter of minutes a pair of Mordagaiian warriors turn a corner. Their crossbows ready for action. Eyes looking for the enemy or sudden movements. Such precautions prove ineffective as both are felled by rebel arrows. Both rebels promptly walk to their mounts in the close by ravine to begin the journey east knowing the main body is but minutes away. Roughly ten minutes later the Mordagi commander finds his men. An angered Mordagi commander turns his men to the east to pursue the attackers. Zandra's mission has been a success.

9

Bloodshed In The Forest Eld

Two days have passed since Badger has left with his band. At a Mordagaiian encampment a rider enters. He quickly informs the commander of that area of their find. A decision is quickly made. The commander sends a message to General Cymon. He knows it will only take two days to place a death cordon around the enemy. The secret of their whereabouts is no longer a secret.

Back at the rebel stronghold Sgt. Cheelo along with his twenty men begin their escort.

"You sure are awful quiet Miranda. Distant in fact."

"My mind thinks of him that is all."

"Badger seems like a fair man. I will wait awhile before passing judgement."

"Never have I met anybody like him Cheelo."

Cheelo looks at Miranda, and gives a assuring nod in response.

A day after Cheelo's unit has left Torman calls a meeting of his remaining sergeants for an emergency meeting.

"It is evident the Mordagi know we are here. Each hour our scouts report more, and more Mordagi approaching from all sides. I suspect a traitor among us. Even before this they were getting awful close."

"Perhaps we should concentrate on their weakest point, and split up for awhile if we manage to break through."

"If they have us truly surrounded we might as well hit their strongest point, and take out as many as we can."

"That is suicide Twistle."

"What is your suggestion than Loptoe!"

"I agree with trying to make a breakthrough in the weakest point. Those of our force successful will have to rendevous at a predetermined location. This means potentially starting from scratch but there is no other choice for us."

The men grow quiet as they look at Torman to hear his decision.

"I am afraid gentlemen that is the only real choice we have. Scouts estimate five hundred already. Not to mention swamp chameleons that are probably in this force. Several dog teams also have been noted. They are probably expecting us to set up defensive positions, and wait for their attack. A quick hitting offensive at their weakest point might just work."

"Where should we regroup at?"

"I think Brigadune would do nicely. Seeing how it lies at the foot of the mountains. Plus it has been deserted for some time now."

"I trust your judgement. When do we commence this plan?"

"Nightfall Loptoe."

"Strategy sounds good."

"One last thing. Say nothing about Brigadune. We must strike quickly, and hard to break through the line. Not until our surviving forces our clear the Eld are they to be informed of Brigadune."

Twistle, and Glite nod in agreement.

At the time of this important battle the Mordagiian force will be at five hundred twenty, four dog teams, and ten swamp chameleons. This is of course their weakest point.

A different type of fighting had begun in the north. A lone Mordagaiian warrior officer rides his mount along Timber trail. As he turns a bend he is felled by arrows. Two forms jump out from behind some dense foliage. Badger then appears. He walks over to the men leading three horses. "Good work men."

"This will get their attention."

"Sure will. The patrol he is attached to should be here any minute. Remember, look surprised. We have got to make them feel they came on us unexpectedly. The others are set."

Minutes later a ten man Mordagi patrol rounds the bend to see three rebels mounting their mounts next to a fallen comrade. Their displeasure over this obvious from their angered looks, and shouts.

"This is it guys. Let's move out. Don't look back."

An order is given, and the Mordagi begin pursuit. The following chase continues for two miles. The trail becomes narrow as the sides get rigid. To the left a straight drop down. On their right walls of dirt, and rock. The Mordagi are suddenly surprised when their adversaries stop ahead of them. Badger draws a concealed sidearm eliminating the first three. Illio, Chingat, and Kolabar quickly seal off the only escape route while taking two more Mordagi fighters in the process. The remaining Mordagiian fighters fall victim to men attacking from camouflaged positions along the dirt wall. Upon completion of the attack the victors quickly retire from the battleground.

That night Badger's band discusses the days event.

"I must admit I was not really sure about you at first, but now I would be willing to follow you to the gates of death."

"I appreciate that Jolo. I am proud to fight along side all of you."

"It will be a glorious day when we defeat the wizard along with his army of minions."

Dorad then proceeds to sit down by the fire not forgetting one final important reminder.

"Oh, by the way. It is time for Ribble to take watch.

Meanwhile a confrontation nears actual combat in the forest of Eld. It is nightfall, and Torman's forces have prepared for an assault against the Mordagi. Torman, along with his remaining sergeants sit on their mounts just out of view of the Mordagi. Their forces spread along a mile long attack line. A line of warriors determined to break through. All fully aware the time to do or die was at hand. Also knowing failure was probably certain death for any chances of the Mordagi ever being defeated.

"The time has come men. This is do or die. If I do not make it Brigadune is still the best place for regrouping. For any of you that do not make it let it be known I hold each of you in the highest regards. Good luck."

A solemn look is exchanged between all. All knowing full well this could be their final action. They disperse to take up places along the line.

Along the Mordagiian front there is an uneasy calm. Every few feet there are archers roaming along with sentries placed indiscriminately amongst the trees. A swamp chameleon disguised as a owl also placed in the trees. Within sight behind these forces is the camp of that sector. Mixed in amongst this are fires, and tents where the bulk of the Mordagiian troops are resting or eating. At the commanders tent he looks over a piece of paper. A smile showing approval of the message.

All of a sudden the quiet night is broken with the sound of horses in a charge. Mordagiian troops begin looking trying to aim with their weapons in that direction. A sentry begins to shout a warning, but receives a fatal blow from a crossbow. He falls from his roost as dozens of riders engage the enemy. The Mordagi are in disarray at first. Surprise has been achieved. Warriors fall from the quick, and decisive attack of the rebels. Some sentries are able to cause losses to the rebels, but are dealt with accordingly. A short distance away where Twistle conducts his part of the fight he encounters some difficulty. A Mordagi fighter has knocked him off his horse. Both draw swords. Unexpectedly another rebel appears out of nowhere, and thrusts his sword into the enemy.

"I don't recognize you friend."

"Killamon Sgt. Twistle, and since your steed took off I suggest you double with me."

"Very well. I accept the offer. Forward with haste to Brigadune."

The momentum is carried as Torman pushes along with his men into the Mordagi sector camp. With the element of surprise starting to fade quickly the Mordagi begin giving stiff resistance. Nearly the first wave of rebels are totally destroyed. Two dogs are let loose to wage war on their terms against the rebels. Three swamp chameleons stand off to the side of the main fighting. As the main body of the rebels continue fierce fighting with the remainder of the camp Torman breaks off with a group to deal with the dogs, and chameleons. They dismount as the dogs charge them. They fire their crossbows with deadly accuracy.

"Where did the swamp chameleons go? Maybe they changed already."

"Not likely Dolp. On our left men. Look out Dolp!"

The warning comes to late as Dolp is hit with a poison orb. Torman, and his men launch a barrage of arrows at the swamp chameleons hoping to hit a vulnerable area. The barrage merely bounces off their hide. A second man goes down near Torman. When Torman had a group of twenty some men break with him to take on the chameleons he figured that would be enough. It did not take long for him to doubt that. Before they swarmed the creatures almost half had already taken orbs, and were deceased. However the plan was working. The close in fighting was messing up their concentration which was vital for them to control the orbs. One swamp chameleon went down from a sword slash in their soft area. The remaining two were holding off the sword blows well. It sounded like metal on metal. In essence it was. After several minutes they finally got wounds inflicted on vulnerable areas, and took them down. Once it was said, and done though Torman only had five left of the twenty. He knew it was going to become imperative they find a way to penetrate their hides. They posed just to great a danger to ignore. The Mordagi loss in that sector was one hundred fifty men, two dogs, three chameleons. Torman had lossed sixty men. Minutes before leaving Torman comes across a piece of paper on the ground. He takes a look. The break through attack was just in time. An all out attack from all sides had been ordered for the coming dawn. Even though he knew they had suffered heavy losses so had the enemy. But the most important thing was that he, and others had broken through. The resistance was still alive. Now it was time to hotfoot it out of there, and reorganize at Brigadune. After seeing his men successfully break through the enemy lines Loptoe gathers what men he can to personally congratulate them. He informs them to go to Brigadune. They acknowledge promptly riding off. Ten minutes later Loptoe indiscreetly happens across a meeting taking place between a swamp chameleon, and a resistance fighter he recognizes. Knivenlaw is the traitor. He decides to wait till they part to act. In just a couple of minutes the chameleon leaves. Knivenlaw watches him till he is out of sight, and sound. As the traitor turns he finds himself facing Loptoe.

"So you have been the traitor all along!"

"Yes. My father is General Cymon. I am a Blackard. Trained to inflict pain for the wizard."

"So the escape from the enslaved town of Egia was a clever lie for us."

"True. Now I will destroy you."

Loptoe takes his knife out of it's sheath. The two combatants circle around each other. With lightning speed Knivenlaw delivers a kick to the chest knocking Loptoe to the ground. He is unable to rise quick enough to avoid a fatal kick to the throat. The secret of Knivenlaw remains a secret. He mounts to rejoin the others unaware yet of where the rebels are going to regroup.

As Torman leads his contingency of men through the land his thoughts are of the men, and women he has sent out. He so much hopes they are being successful on their assignments. Such concerns can only drain the energy from a commander. Yet the journey westward continues.

In the town of Olo one of those assignments has went well. As three men sitting at a table amongst the crowds of Olo watch a small Mordagi patrol pass through the town they feel contentment. Success was achieved.

"It appears the hounds have lost the fox. Better go to the inn to inform Zandra."

"Okay Chind. The way should be clear for us to go back now."

Gruno walks in among the crowds till he reaches the inn. He proceeds to one of the upper rooms. Stopping at one of the doors he looks around before knocking. A feminine voice is heard in reply.

"Who calls on this afternoon?"

"It is Gruno."

The door slowly opens. zandra is gathered with four more of the fighters in the room. "What news do you have?"

"Good news. The patrol has passed with no apparent idea who was behind the attack on their scouts."

"Good. That means we shall return to camp. Have the men assemble two miles outside of town at nightfall."

Elsewhere a separate group reach the base of the Shastle mountains. The men become more high spirited as the end of their trek grows near. Unknown to them a lone wolf spies their movement. The red eyed wolf quietly leaves the area. Miranda feels a sudden chill down her spine.

"What is wrong?"

"I felt like we were being watched Cheelo."

Nervous eyes quickly survey in all directions. Nothing seems wrong.

"The feeling is gone. It must not have been anything."

"Perhaps. Take four men, and check the area around us Kilpa. We will wait here."

"Yes sir!"

Kilpa quickly points to four men who fall out of the group. They break from the group to search in a circular pattern. Fifteen minutes later they reappear. Kilpa reports.

"Nothing to report sir. Checked in all directions."

"Very well. Let's proceed."

Days later a very enraged wizard meets his cabinet in the council chambers. The wizard, many of his generals, a visionist, and two blackards are present.

"We have lost almost three hundred from the preemptive strike the rebels took along with these raids on our small patrols. We were in a position to totally destroy them, and instead we took losses we should not have. We also have to start over finding those who got away. Enough of that though. Why haven't you found the raiders who are ripping up our patrols General Cymon?"

"They keep moving around. They only attack small patrols. Our tactics are not geared for this type of fighting."

"I am not interested in excuses. Enlarge all patrols from now on. This should hold them at bay. General Bishop."

"Yes master."

"Someone must pay for our losses. Since you allowed him to come here it is only fitting that you be the one. Blackards! Dismember him leaving a limb hanging at each corner of the fortress. Toss the head into the swamp."

A surprised General makes a futile attempt to resist as the Blackards drag him off to his fate.

The Generals exit. The visionist speaks.

"Badger is the key. Destroy him, and you crush the movement. If not he will crush you."

"He is not even of this place. How can he be my downfall?"

"He has been picked by the forces of good to stop you. Not even he is aware of this."

"I will figure a way to destroy him. No one is invincible."

The wizard then silently leaves the room. The words of the visionist still fresh in his mind.

The time for Badger along with his men to return has arrived.

"I have gathered you all here tonight so that I can let you know we start back tomorrow afternoon to rejoin the main body. A good nights rest to you all."

The group breaks up. Jot notices Badger walk into the woods. He silentle follows. Badger stops at the edge of a creek. Jot walks up next to him.

"It is going to be good to be back with the others. Thanks to you we are going to turn the tide."

"It is not me Jot. You, and those like you who stand up against tyranny together make the difference. I only do my part in this fight."

"You have showed us a lot."

"Before you go back there is something I have to tell you. I want you to take the men back for me. There is something I must do. It could take awhile. Tell Miranda I love her in case you see her before I do."

"You sound worried. You should not travel by yourself. It is not a wise choice for someone still unfamiliar with the land. Let me go with you."

"I'll be fine really. I just want to find somebody."

"You are going to go look for Kanessa aren't you?"

He is answered with silence.

"I am going with you regardless of what you say."

"You are a very stubborn man Jot."

A stern face is replaced with a wide grin.

"Glad to have you."

"One question though Badger. How do you propose to find her? She is only found when she wants to be."

"I must try."

"Very well."

The following afternoon they watch as the others set off to rejoin the main group. Illio in the lead with tempory command until they get there.

Upon completing this task they begin their quest. It takes days to reach the mountains. They enter the mountains some fifty miles north of Brigadune. Elsewhere a rebel post has been established by Cheelo. Jot becomes more intrigued by Badger's description of his world as he presses him to talk about it.

"There were no evil wizards where you come from."

"No. Plenty of very bad people who over our history had to be stopped though. There is something I wondered about you can probably answer for me."

"I will if I can."

"What did Torman do before the war?"

"He farmed a piece of land near the Liber with his family."

"I did not realize he had a family. Where are they now?"

"One day before the Mordagi sent the main invasion force he sent out assasins, and small bands to strike at certain people who he thought would be trouble. Torman was gone on business when his place got hit. He returned to find his wife, and son Carb murdered. He even has a bounty on his head by the Mordagi. He later found out it was also when the sisterhood was attacked. In less than a week

Torman had organized the resistance. It is said a visionist supplied the list of those attacked."

"It is getting late Jot. This will be a good place for camp."

The next morning at the fortress a discussion is under way between the wizard, and General Cymon.

"The best opportunity for us to get the orange eye that we have had has presented itself. I know where it is. It is guarded by a handful of men. Miranda is also among them. Take what you need. Bring me the orange eye along with Miranda. She may prove useful. Destroy the rest."

"You wish me to lead the mission?"

"Yes. This is to important to let fail. With the eye in my possesion I will know where the rebels are at all times. No longer will I have to depend on spies. We will be able to wipe them out where they prepare instead of wasting time searching for them."

Cymon bows as he makes his leave. That afternoon three Blackards, three chameleons, and fifty Mordagi troops leave the fortress.

Elsewhere, from a crevice in the mountain side a lone figure observes two riders proceed further into the mountains. A closer look reveals them as Badger, and Jot.

"The horses need some rest. The ground is starting to level out some. How about here?"

"Not bad thinking Jot. It will not hurt to exercise our legs either."

"How about letting me shoot your weapons?"

Badger dismounts to casually inspect the immediate area. Satisfied he walks back to his horse to remove the saddle. His gentle hands pat the horses neck as he calmly speaks.

"Good boy. Time for some rest."

"Let me shoot the weapons."

"I am not sure if it is a good idea. Suppose you are heard."

"The Mordagi stay out of the mountains."

"Well. It would be nice to have fresh meat. Okay. Bring back what you can, meanwhile I am going to get a fire going."

"Sure thing. Be back soon with some good eating."

Jot walks from sight. Badger goes about collecting wood. When Jot returns a fine conflagration is burning. He returns with a big smile. Slung over his back a rope with several hares tied to it. Badger ushers forth a question.

"How many?"

"Four. This is going to be good eating."

"The change is most welcome."

Night has started to take it's place as Badger looks up to the stars. Badger sees a picture of Miranda in his mind. He longs to see, and hold her again. He hopes her safety is still well. Off to his side Jot has begun preparing the evening meal. When the feasting is done they converse before getting some sleep.

"If we do not find her soon we are going to have no choice but to return empty handed."

"Just remember what I said about how hard she is to find. You are giving it the best effort you can."

"Thanks Jot, but that does not make me feel any better. I hate failure."

A hawk circles above them. It glides in among the tree tops like a kite would. Unnoticed it flies a short distance away to a figure with an outstretched arm. The figure is in a flowing robe which hides the identity of this individual. This secrecy is helped also with the accompanying hood. The outstretched arm does have a delicate appearance to it though.

At the rebel camp now positioned at Brigadune Sergeant Twistle, and Torman discuss the absence of Loptoe. Weeks have passed with no signs of him."

"I fear that something has happened to him."

"It does not make any sense Twistle. A group of men directly under his command saw him after the fighting. They even talked to him. What could have happened to him?"

"Perhaps he was followed. I have to admit I think he is dead. For this reason I feel we should appoint another sergeant."

"Any suggestions?"

"Killamon Roli. He is a very good fighter."

"Done. I still hold out hope Loptoe will be back with us."

"I know you two have gone through alot together. I also hope for the best."

Torman can only look at his comrade with saddened eyes. He quietly walks to his tent.

10

Kanessa Found

The following morning a sunrise of grandeur greets Badger, and Jot as they awaken. The sun makes the mountains look alive. Badger can't help but comment.

"Boy what a beaut."

Jot notices the horses acting peculiar. He walks over to the saddles that are laying on the ground. He then bends down, and picks up a .45 auto from a side pouch. Badger puts his hand on the handle of the .38 which is on the gunbelt he is wearing. The horses are only about ten feet away from them. They start to jerk wildly. Jot begins to advance cautiously. Badger takes his firearm completely out of it's holster. The horses are tethered to a rope tied between two trees. There is a thick tree line. The horses break free as a grizzly bear of immense size thunders forward. The creature's razor sharp claws, and sudden attack throw Jot off balance. The grizzly outstretches a paw, and throws Jot several feet threw the air. He lands with a sickening thud. His weapon falling where he stood just seconds before. The grizzly lumbers forward. A haphazard shot by Badger nicks the right shoulder of the beast. Badger takes several steps backward. The bear stands on his hind feet, and lets out a loud growl. It then continues an advance. Badger looks over to where Jot is. His figure still limp on the ground. In his retreat Badger tries to take aim for the next shot. The shot goes well to the left of the grizzly. Seizing the opportunity he jumps on the off balanced Badger. The bear sensing victory sends a claw tearing into the left side of his opponent. Badger feels an unimaginable heat course through his body. He knows death is looking over him with a sinister smile. Even so he grips hold of some fur under the jaw line. The bear becomes erect for a second time. Badger drops to crawl towards a ravine that lies within ten feet. Without mercy a claw draws blood on his right side. Badger finally goes still ready to accept the end when two timber wolves appear from the woods. The snarling teeth cause the grizzly to turn to face his new challengers. Without fear the newcomers start circling the mammoth. Claws slash out in defiance for being interrupted. Using the new time supplied to him Badger painstakingly makes it to the ravine, and quickly slides down it. Once reaching the bottom he loses consciuosness.

When Badger awakes he sees a beautiful woman sitting over him. Short blond hair braided at the top. Eyes hazel with very slender curving cheekbones. She was wearing clothing that covered her chest quite sufficiently yet revealed enough to make any healthy man want to see more. Actually even a man ill probably would want to see more. Since Badger was laying on what was evidently a bed that was the only observations he could make of her. Even at this point though he could already be confident he was hoping to expand this assesment. His wounds had been dressed, and bandaged. A single candle was burning in the center of the room on a small wooden table. Also placed there were his weapons, and clothing. By the door a timber wolf was standing guard quietly. With a pleasing voice she speaks to Badger.

"You are going to be alright. It will take a few weeks for your injuries to fully heal, but they should. I have been watching you for quite awhile as you made your journey up through the mountains. Where is your destination?"

"I am looking for somebody. Possibly you."

"Who do you think I am? Who do you hold an alliance with?"

"I fight for what is right. The Mordagi threaten your entire world. I think you realize this. You are Kanessa aren't you? I am here to enlist your help."

"I said nothing. You could be a Blackard for all I know. Spies are everywhere. Why should I beleive you?"

"The time for you to beleive someone has come. Those who fight this evil need your help."

"Are you hungry Badger?"

"Yes. Was there anything you could do for my friend?"

"I'm afraid not. Please beleive me when I say I wish we would have got to you sooner. His neck was broken in two places.

You have been in a deep slumber for three days now. I did bury him during that time. I hope that does not upset you."

"No. That was the answer I expected. That was a proper thing to do for him. Thank you. By the way his name was Jot."

Kanessa quietly goes about cooking some meat. Her quietness leaves Badger wondering if a nerve has been hit with any of his words.

11

Reunion Of The Bold

In the ghost town of Brigadune which has been reverted into a rebels post a group of five riders appear. They are halted by sentries placed high amongst some trees. Torman rides up with three more men to investigate. As Torman recognizes them he feels joy as he finds out they are his men.

The men whom are present are Ribble, Jolo, Illio, Kolabar, and Crale. The men are quiet for a minute. Ribble is the first to utter a word.

"So this is where you disappeared to. We have been looking for you for quite some time now."

Torman becomes increasingly concerned with the fact none of the other men who should be present materialize.

"Where are the other men?"

Illio prods his mount to the front. Looking directly at Torman he answers trying to hold back bitterness without much success.

"Dead. Killed in fighting that took place in the forest of Eld. In the area our camp was suppose to be. Remember. All except Badger, and Jot. They took off for a journey into the mountains. He said he would catch up in a few days."

Fighting to hold back his emotions Torman instructs Illio to meet him after he has settled in. Torman pulls his reigns back, and gallops off. The men remaining escort the tired band to their new quarters. The riders pass between dozens of clay brick buildings. As they near the opposite side of town they see greater numbers of men milling about. The escort stops the procession in front of a two story structure. There are few windows visible. Just beyond that a stable has been rejuvenated. Four sentries are visible. One of the escort riders leads his horse over to Illio.

"Here you go sir. There should be plenty of room for all of you. Torman's tent is just inside the tree line along the trail. Before we go we just want to say it is good to have you back."

The escort departs. The men dismount. Getting their saddle rolls they enter their new quarters. Illio meets with Torman that evening.

"Would you like a drink?"

"No. I just want to know what happened at camp after we left. We hit road block after road block in the Eld. I did not enjoy losing those men like I did especially when I thought I was back in friendly territory."

"A short time after you embarked on the mission Mordagaiian forces with superior numbers began to encircle the Eld where we were at. It became evident at that time we have a spy amongst us. In a concentrated effort we struck at their weakest point we could find managing to break through. All the while we kept are destination a secret till we were safely away. I imagine you have noticed our numbers are somewhat smaller. We did take losses, but enough of that. How did the mission go? What kind of effect did you have or could you see any at all?"

"A success. We bled the enemy. They have been forced to use more forces to secure even the patrols."

"I see. Badger taught you well."

"Yes. We inflict greater injury to the enemy than they are able to reciprocate immediately. It's at least something while we continue to marshal up forces."

"What was Badger's explanation for the trip into the mountains.?"

"He would not be specific."

Torman becomes silent. He paces for a minute. As he rubs his chin a thought comes to mind.

"Of course. I bet he is searching for Kanessa. I must admit one thing about the man. Once he gets an idea he doesn't let loose of it. I hope he finds her."

"A few minutes ago you mentioned we have a spy. Any ideas."

"Unfortunately not. But he is here."

"What are you going to do?"

A grim faced Torman answers.

"I do not know."

As the conversation ends a different takes place in the mountains.

"That was a fine meal. I'm starting to feel better. In a few days it will be time for me to leave to join back up with the main rebel force."

"That's to soon Badger. The riding alone will slow down the healing of your ribs. You give it two more weeks. By then you should be ready."

Badger starts to sit up but feels tearing in stitches followed by some pain. He decides to lay back down.

"I suppose I could stay a little longer. I really wish you would accompany me. The time to make the Mordagi face retribution is coming. You could help make it happen."

"Let me tell you a story Badger. There was a time I was in love with a Mordagi warrior named Igadrom. He was a kind loving man. He stayed true to that right up to his death. On the night the Mordagi began their murderous onslaught Igadrom was with the group assigned to attack the sisterhood. When they got the orders he bolted in hopes of reaching us to warn us of the danger. He made it about halfway before he was stopped. I was one of few to escape. I found him myself. He was actually still alive. In his last breaths he told me of a list of targets the royal family had told the wizard to see wiped out early on. That is why I stay away. As far as I know the first strikes were a success for them. I'm on the list. If I stay out of it maybe I can convince them I am dead to."

"Do you really think this place is safety? Your loss is great but so are many others. My friend Jot died helping me try to find you. The evil that threatens your world will not go away unless it is destroyed. As we speak another like you is helping in the fight. Miranda is not off hiding in some fantasy world like you are. Eventually this place will also fall under their control. It's just a matter of time. There are no true safe havens anymore."

"Miranda is still alive?"

"Yes."

"You should rest. We can talk later."

With that Kanessa quietly makes her way outside.

12

Floodgates Are Opened

In the Mordagi capital of Grandago Emperor Gitch meets with his inner circle. For the occasion the wizard has traveled to attend by request of Gitch himself. Also present our his two sons Sipian, and cutnuts. Making up the remainder our as follows Coffle head of internal security for the royal family, Vantrox supreme Blackard, and finally Warchuck Supreme commander of the armed forces. Only one family member was kept out of these things, and that was Gitch's daughter Shebith. The reason for this will become more obvious as we proceed.

"I have good news to pass on to you all. Our wizard Hob informs me the orange eye should be ours within days. He has located where it is. They have a small force protecting it. Evidently they figured we would be to busy in the Eld to also continue the search for it simultaneously."

"Those who oppose us by now should know it is hopeless. We have finished our work in the Eld, and the last of the Covehi territories. It is now ours. Those suitable for the slave camps have begun orientation."

"Supreme commander Warchuck has any of the last sisterhood been found during this."

"Not at this time. The four still unaccounted for shall not stay that way. I also am ready to start the next phase on your orders majesty."

"The count is actually about to go to three. I forgot to say Miranda is with the eye. The others will still need to be found. My sons grow tired of waiting for their wives."

"They should be kept away from the royal family emperor."

"Now see here Coffle. As we discussed before my sons have taken notice of them. Once they have children their special abilities will be gone. My sons will keep them in line."

"You should probably also know the orders have been put out that all those 12 through 18 are to begin military schooling by order of the Emperor."

"Very good Warchuck. It is time to launch offensive action beyond the Covehi. Initiate action on the Argonnes. My son Sipian will lead a force against the Hykolites."

"As you order our legions will leave within the hour. Long live the great one."

Upon this the session comes to an end, and as one could say the hounds of hell are cut loose. The Covehi had been dealing with but a fraction of what the Emperor had been assembling. In the parade grounds of Grandago a force of 30,000 troops had been waiting for just that command. That evening the force made up of 20,000 mounted troops, 10,000 archers in wagons head west to broaden their hold. Riders sent ahead will reach General Cymon two days ahead of the main forces to inform him of the reinforcements, and new orders. The following day Sipian will lead a force of 15,000 troops who will attack the Hykolite capitol. It is the only town they have that has much of a population. They also have no standing army.

13

Miranda In Jeopardy

Miranda opens her eyes feeling something awry. It is three in the morning. She begins to whisper to Cheelo who is close by in the same cave when the assault is launched. The five perimeter guards go down quickly. Most of the rest of the defenders do manage to grab their weapons laying next to them to offer futile resistance. Four men fall back to the cave entrance as Torman steps out. The regular Mordagi troops encircle the remaining men at the entrance. Three Blackards step through the cordon. In amazing speed one throws a knife which penetrates the throat of one of their targets. Torman glances over as his comrade goes to the ground. Miranda is then heard as she steps out to stand next to Torman, and whats left of the escort.

"Wait. No more. We will lay down our weapons just don't kill these men."

Cheelo looks at her in a uncertain way.

"You and these men have done everything you possibly could. What will the last four of you dying do for the cause. If they will agree to take you prisoner at least you will be alive. What do you say Blackards?"

One Blackard starts to take a step forward, but is stopped by another as he puts his hand on his chest.

"We will take these leftovers prisoner. I have my reasons. Put your weapons on the ground, and step away from them."

The men look at Cheelo. He concludes meaningless deaths serve no purpose, and throws down his sword. The men follow suit defiantly.

Within two weeks they will be at the prison camp just outside the fortress awaiting their final disposition. The charming name of this place is Ohno.

14

Back In The Fight

Unknown to Badger just days before Miranda's capture he has started his journey back out of the mountains. To his releif Kanessa has decided to make the journey. He knows her decision was not easy. He had gained a respect as he watched her give final farewells to the timber wolves she had grown very attached to. Kanessa had even turned away from Badger to hide several tears.

The trip was giving Badger the feel of a recreational affair until he came across the remains of Cheelo's men. The realization of what this meant quickly hit him as if a pike was being jabbed in his chest. He carefully surveyed everything several times. He knew the orange eye was not there. He could only imagine what was happening to his love. Deep in his heart he had to fight the truth that he might not see her alive again. It was late in the day when they happened across this so they set up camp close by. Even though Kanessa had cooked rabbit over the fire Badger just could not eat. Instead his thoughts were only of Miranda. He had sworn to himself he would not let anything happen to her, and he had failed.

Sitting by the fire Kanessa could see the pain Badger was trying to work through. She sat next to him, and placed an arm around him. Badger rested his head against her breasts. Listening to her heartbeat he let her warmth cascade over him. He falls into a much needed sleep. Kanessa knows the pain he suffers, and can only hope that a safe return may still happen.

Elsewhere Illio accomapanied by Kalip, Ribble, and Goosbe doing a short patrol on the western side of Brigadune have noticed an armed band of maybe 30 fighters coming out of the mountains.

"I don't know about you men but from here they look different then the Mordagi."

"I'm not sure what to think Illio. They have banners with markings I have never seen before. What about you Goosbe? You are new to the fight. Familiar at all?"

"When I was a young boy my father took me to land in the Argonnes territory. When we can make out the colors of those banners I can tell for sure. Green with a red circle is the colors of the military, and seal of their High councilor."

"Kalip, go find Torman. Report this immediately."

"You got it Illio."

"How long do you think it will take them to get here Ribble?"

"Twenty minutes."

"If they are unfriendlies I am not going down without one hell of a fight. I don't see any point in trying to take off."

"I am with you all the way Illio."

After the new arrivals have made it over half way to Illio's group exuberance can be seen on their faces. The banners are indeed Argonnes. More detail reveals they also wear green tunics with patches on the left shoulders bearing crossed sabers above a horses head. All of them with rather impressive swords to boot. Having spotted Illio, and those with him they proceeded right up to them maintaining a set formation. Illio could not help but remark to the others just how disciplined they came off. As the first words were about to be spoken Torman showed up with about twenty men. He held the twenty men back as soon as he saw them.

"You men hold here. I do beleive help may be knocking on our back door."

Torman casually rides up the rest of the way to his patrol.

The Argonean commander directly looks at Torman.

"I am Hixen commander specially commisioned by the High Councilor. We are on a intelligence hunt. We are not here to offend the Covehi. Perhaps you could tell us who you are."

"Torman. I lead the fight against the Mordagi. Early on I sent one of the best riders I had to send a plea for help to the Argonnes. It is my hope that is why you are here."

"We never received that plea. A handful of reports from a few who made it through the mountains have made it to our leader however. Everything we have heard says that without reason or provocation of any kind they started a war with you. My duty is to confirm what is going on, and report back directly to the High Councilor."

"So Morot never got to you?"

"Sorry about your man Torman."

"He was a good man. We have lost so many like him. The faces of them start to blur after awhile."

"They have been slaughtering our people. This area around Brigadune is all we have left of our homeland. If there is any decency among you you will not turn your backs to us."

"Illio! I think that will be enough."

Illio ashamed of the outburst sheepishly looks down as Torman continues.

"We really do need your help Hixen. Nothing says the Mordagi are done if they finish us off. Your people could well be next."

"I understand your problem. As far as we know though this could just be a border conflict between you, and the Mordagi."

"A border conflict. Did you hear that Torman. He said this is just a simple border conflict. That's a releif I mean they are only trying to take the Covehi off the face of Statureo itself. I mean what's a little genocide amongst neighbors. Next he'll say it's just a misunderstanding!"

"That's enough Illio! Take your patrol back to camp. I mean now mister."

Illio, Kalip, Ribble, and Goosbe who was amongst those who returned with Torman left.

"Ok Torman. My High Councilor did give me some discretion. I will offer your forces along with any innocents in your care safe passage through the mountains to just inside our land under our banners. We shall see if the Mordagi violate our territorial integrity also. If they do we have an alliance. I will make sure I have every possible approach monitored by my scouts. If they cross I will know in hours. Once we get to the other side of the mountains reinforcements should be arriving."

"Reinforcements? Sounds like you have already reached a decision before you got here."

"No decision. We just don't plan on being caught unprepared."

"We will accept the honorable offer. Thank you."

"we will go back to your camp with you. We will give you two days to prepare for the journey. At that time we go with or without you. I will need to get a report headed back quickly."

"Understood. We will be ready to move out."

In the land of the Sanders it has come time to introduce a character who will become an important contributor to the war effort although he does not know this yet. He is known as Fluffy the metalsmith, and a very fine one indeed. He has a mischievous apprentice named Snackle. His choosing was of no particular reason other than it just seemed right.

Fluffy was known to make many decisions this way. There were more than a few who thought him to be odd however the common answer to this was that's just Fluffy. One thing all agreed on was that he was the best metalsmith around. He had learned well from his father Flambian.

Fluffy was a Sander who lived in the town of Horganpoes Ring. It is said the founding father's were led by Horganpoe thus receiving the honor. The family tree of the Sanders was somewhat questionable. This group was originally a large band of thieves, con artists, and the like. They were run out of their birthplace in the west.

Around this time Fluffy has found a new metal in several places in the Drosch desert. He has even given it a name. Bormitian. Unknown to him at this point he has found what will become the best defense against the swamp chameleons. This individual has short, black hair, brown eyes, usually a couple days worth of stubble, and a body frame close to a brick wall.

15

Mordagi Expansion

The Hykolites fall in a matter of days. Being along the northern coast they are a simple people living off of the sea. They were ignorant of what they considered the outside world. Even when a small band of riders showed up warning of impending doom they were basically ignored. This unfortunately put them at a loss of words when Sipian rode in with his force. Most of the general population which was about 3000 had gathered in the middle of town. Sipian wasted no time in showing his ruthlessness. The Mordagi forces quickly encircled the population. Sipian opened up with a chilling declaration.

"To the Hykolites. As of now you no longer exist. You are now slaves under the Mordagi banner, and subjects of the royal family. You no longer need to worry about rights of any kind for you have none. Nonobediance will not be tolerated."

For the first time the Hykolites were going to know true terror. Without hesitation he gave a hand signal to a contingent of men that had moved slightly away from the rest of the force. A deadly salvo of arrows rained into the mass of people. The assault takes a toll of 220. The Hykolites are forced to submit.

"Commander, I will leave a contingent of one thousand behind. Take a torch to anything that burns. Add to the prisoner count if you can. Remember though. Tolerate no resistance. Upon completion of this task reinforce the garrison at Morril."

"As you command Sipian."

"My father will be pleased with our victorious return."

As Sipian readies his return the wizard Hob has returned to his fortress to discuss plans with General Cymon along with a handful of other key commanders.

"Well Cymon. The Emperor is expecting great strides in a short time. All the lands between the Shastle mountains, and the homeland except for a portion of the snake river including Brigadune is ours. It was their last refuge. It is unfortunate that we now have again sufficient force to finish the Covehi off but now will also have to deal with the Argonnes. I have become aware through my abilities they have started going on a war footing. The surprise we wanted will not be there. As the forces you have approaching Brigadune from the north along the mountain base, entering Brigadune from the east, and forces coming up along the snake river will find out when they converge on Brigadune."

Amongst the gathered is a younger Mordagi commander named Sparole. He shows no hesitation in joining the discussion.

"So be it. It's not like we are stopping at the mountain range anyway. We now have the entire Covehi lands. At Ohno we have almost one thousand prisoners who will prove good slaves for us. Those who are thought to have any connection with the resistance are interrogated by Blackards then disposed of. The Argonnes are a stronger opponent this is true, but they will still fall under us."

"Yes Sparole your administration of the camp has been very well done. Do make sure you remember not to kill off Miranda along with her entourage. Gitch wants them to, when the time is right, sent to Grandago for final disposition. Since we are on the subject you still have three from the sisterhood not accounted for Cymon."

"The Blackards using their methods at Ohno have good reason to beleive she is in the mountains. A Covehi in a dying declaration said the resistance is pretty sure of that. Evidently she continues isolation."

A third general utters a question.

"Any intelligence on the whereabouts of this Badger"

The wizard Hob is slow to answer but eventually does.

"This Badger you speak of has proven to be quite elusive. I for quite some time now have lost any awareness of him. If he was dead I would have had a sense the threat was gone. This is not the case."

Hob is interrupted by General Cymon. An evident irritation is held back.

"You have always said death, and the sisterhood were the only things that could mask themselves against you. This makes no sense."

"There is one scenario which does."

"So just what would that be Sparole?"

"Badger has found at least one of our missing sisterhood. That's how he is being masked."

"Very good Sparole. That is indeed my conclusion also. General Cymon our main forces will be in Brigadune in 24 hours. In three days from now you are to push into the mountains, and as swiftly as possible secure them. Engagement of the Argonnes will quickly follow."

"As you command."

The meeting breaks up until Hob is alone with General Cymon.

"Before you go general I want to discuss your son. It has been several months now, and yet it appears he has not completed his assignment. His target is still breathing."

"I know Hob. Knivenlaw will succeed. He was not decorated by Vantrox for being a failure."

"I hold faith you are correct, and that we will see results soon. One last thing. I have sent word to Vantrox to send a contingent of Blackards into the mountains north of our forces to specifically look for Badger."

The following day somewhere between the Hykolite capital, and Shastle mountain range a group of riders are found being pursued by Mordagiian troops. Numerically they are at a disadvantage. A closer look reveals it to be Zandra's missing band. They are currently heading west pushing their horses as fast as they will go. For the most part they have open range for the time being. The pursuers well in sight.

"Don't they ever get tired!"

"You go right ahead and ask them while the rest of us keep heading out Trulip."

"I think I will pass but just our luck to get a patrol of some fifty men though."

In moments the appearance of a creek starts to loom ahead. Not a huge water obstacle but enough to slow down their speed while crossing. They go down a embankment of three feet. As they conduct the crossing many of their mounts show signs of exhaustion. Trulip is the first to reach the opposite side. Zandra along with three others just seconds later. Trulip quickly makes it up out of the creekbed first. His steed only goes a couple of steps before he pulls back on the reigns. The horse kicks up in protest. The rest have finished the crossing. Zandra sees Trulip stop, and starts to say something.

"What the hell do you think you are do . . . ?"

She knows there are no words to properly describe the pain they are about to experience. For on the horizon for as far as the eyes can see a Mordagi army of thousands is on the move. A mixture of cavalry, and wagons loaded with troops. As she looks behind them everyone has made the crossing while the pursuers are practically at the opposite bank. Pointing back across the water Zandra utters a single statement.

"The time has come to accept our fate. May the Covehi never be extinguished."

With those words she starts back down to meet the enemy in the creek bed. The rest show no hesitation in following suit. They meet the Mordagi head on at the waters edge. All but fifteen of the Mordagi descend to engage in the close quarter combat. As they pull their crossbows out it is evident they plan to snipe at their opponents from the high ground. Zandra gets the first kills as she masterfully uses her sword on two of the enemy. The fight is fierce as Gruno uses himself to dislodge a Mordagi officer off his mount. Three of the Covehi go down from mortal hits. They are pushed into the water, and quickly find themselves encircled. Trulip slashes three to their demise when he gets thrown from his mount. Digart dives off his mount to try to give Trulip some cover in the knee deep water. As Gruno finishes off the officer with a cut to the upper leg he is hit in the back by three arrows. He gives a gasp as he falls face down next to the Mordagi officer whose blood still gushes from the femoral artery. Tisnot manages to have his sword knocked out of his grasp so he lunges on the back of a enemy mount. The Mordagi rider tries to shake him off but has no luck as Tisnot delivers strong jabs to his ribcage. Unfortunately he receives help as a comrade delivers a fatal head wound to Tisnot who falls lifeless into the water. Meanwhile Trulip was quick to get up to press the fight alongside Digart from a standing position. Zandra's mount has been fatally taken down some twenty feet away. The remaining two Covehi manage to get alongside her. Two more Mordagi fall as they do so. As Trulip dismounts two more opponents go down. Digart takes a sword hit right through the chest. A horse rearing up knocks Trulip unconscious. Chind and Norkel bravely try to take the pressure off Zandra as she attempts to saddle up again without success. She feels a slash to her left at the same time a sword hilt strikes her on the right side of the cheek. She goes limp. Chind along with Norkel manage to eliminate eight Mordagi before they too fall for good.

Several hours pass before Zandra awakens to find herself lying on a stretcher. She can feel bandages around her side. A visible bruise evident on her right cheek. She makes an attempt to move her hands but finds they are restrained to her sides. She has the sense of movement, and realizes she is in a wagon. The only other survivor of the fight finds himself in the same situation in the next wagon directly behind Zandra's.

16

United Again With Vital Knowledge

It has become known that a miniscule percentile of the Covehi population fled towards the Argonnes for sanctuary. Using countless trails of varying difficulty to accomplish this. On one of these so called trails we find a oddity. A simple traveler who is making a similiar journey. He is in his late twenties with a plump figure. Unfortunately he has stumbled across three theives. One of these gents is holding the reigns of their horses along with the traveler's while the other two conduct business. One has his right hand on his sword hilt while the other holds a knife close to their prey.

"For the last time. Leave all your possesions right here in a pile, and start walking."

The individual realizes his only real option is to accept defeat. With the look of disappointment he starts to do just that. Unexpectedly a voice is heard.

"What do we have here? Some kind of moral fiber holding you back from killing him."

"Perhaps you should move along with your companion before we decide we want something."

"Maybe you should come closer it is hard to hear manure."

"You are going to regret interfering."

Two fully draw swords as they encroach on Badger. In seconds they are dead. Badger draws one of his firearms firing almost point

71

blank into them. Two shots into their chests each. The third puzzled over what he just witnessed hops on a saddle to gallup away as fast as he can. Once he is no longer seen or heard Badger notices the stranger with a look of concern evident.

"You can relax now stranger. I can assure you I am not of the same cloth as that filth. I am Badger, and this is Kanessa."

"I am in your debt sir. My name is Rolph Cramjelly."

Kanessa interjects a question to Cramjelly.

"You are not Covehi?"

"No my lovely your suspicions are correct. I am of Mordagi nationality."

"Perhaps I was hasty after all when I interceded on your behalf."

"Now hold on Badger. I have no wish to be caught up in this war my people started. I am simply trying to find a place to sit it out. My people are under a control they do not even realize."

At this point the two riders begin dismounting as Badger remarks on that statement.

"I find that hard to believe. Those which I have encountered seem to be working under their own free wills. What makes you say that?"

"Months ago I was witness to the arrival from space of something. It was either glass or diamond material. I am pretty confident it was red. Unfortunately I did not get as close a look at it like I would have liked because the local militia had gotten there just prior to my arrival. They were quick in securing the area. I have not seen or heard about it since that night. Days later the mystical Hob started the Archaic temple of the Brethren with full support of the royal family.

Only himself with a handful of his visionaries as they have become known can enter. The place is also protected by Coffle's special internal security force. In a matter of weeks there were already changes in the attitudes of our leaders wanting to attack those around us. The only reason given was that Statureo would be better ruled under one flag, one royal family. I could imagine what was probably going to happen. The day I started this journey the war started that night. At that point my people had progressed to simply wanting absolute power. Talk of the Mordagi being a chosen race had become the ultimate truth. Their is indeed a force at work here using my people to conduct this slaughter. It is that which I saw."

"You are telling me your entire people are under the control of this so called red diamond? Where are you telling me it is being kept at then Rolph. This Archaic temple . . ."

"It makes the most sense. The timetable of all this is just to perfect. If this influence could be stopped it would end."

Badger goes quiet as he gives careful thought to this newly acquired information. A few minutes later he looks at Kanessa.

"Did the sisterhood feel the orange eye was a object of some kind or a living organism?"

"It could not communicate to us however we felt there was a life energy to it."

"I have a theory Kanessa. If it is true about this other diamond being able to control that means to me it is alive. If something is alive it can be killed. We have got to get back with Torman as soon as possible. How about you Cramjelly. Would you like to join us."

"You will have to excuse me Badger, but I will stick to my original plan. I will find someplace to stay out of it."

"If that is your wish. Considering the time this seems like a good place to rest for the night. You can stay with us for the evening if you wish."

Rolph Cramjelly graciously accepts the offer. The next morning they separate to embark upon their different paths.

"Goodbye Mr. Cramjelly, I wish you luck."

"I wish the same to you two also."

"I am a little bit surprised you wished him luck Kanessa considering he is a Mordagi."

"I think he was telling the truth. The true enemy may not be the Mordagi."

"Maybe. It is hard to see the difference though when you still have to go through them to get to the real enemy if that is the case."

Badger detects sadness in Kanessa's expression.

"If it makes you feel any better I'm leaning towards beleiving that diamond is the cause of all this too."

He notes a smile replace the saddened face. A little later on that day they come across what appears to be an exodus of Covehi making their way through the mountains. He realizes scattered among the procession are groups with banners he does not recognize. Kanessa has no problem on this matter however.

"Badger, those are Argonnes troops. Red circle with a green background."

"The Covehi must have got the Argonnes to ally with them while I was gone. There is something not good though because they are going the wrong way."

As Badger starts to question what he is observing he recognizes voices he has not heard for several weeks. They ride up to him relieved to see he is still alive. Illio, Ribble, and Kolabar make up this spirited welcoming committee. Illio is the first to engage in conversation.

"It is so good to see you. You have probably figured out things are still not going well."

"I am a little lost on what to think. Looks like a retreat but do I see Argonnes troops among you."

"Yes. We are no longer alone in this fight. On their side of the mountains the Argonnes have begun massing troops. We are regrouping there. After you left we got hit hard in the Eld. By the way where is Jot?"

Badger starts to answer but finds the words hard to speak. Kanessa answers for him.

"Your friend died by the hands of a grizzly. It was so quick I doubt he even felt anything."

The men are quiet as they all picture their buddy in their minds. Ribble is the next to talk.

"Where were you at when this happened Badger? Any connection with where you found her."

"Shut up Ribble. Even you should have figured out who she is. He found Kanessa."

"That is a very interesting thought Illio. Why do you say that's who I am."

"Torman figured Badger took off looking for you. He succeeded didn't he."

Badger has managed to regain his composure.

"Yes Illio I was successful. I have also gained some very important information. Where is Torman? There is much I must talk to him about."

"He insisted on personally taking care of the rear guard. At the most they should only be three miles behind us. He has the Argonnes commander with him also."

"I will meet up with you later that's where were headed next."

Badger with Kanessa alongside breakaway from the others to go locate Torman. As they move out of earshot Illio decides perhaps he should go along also. He denies to Ribble, and Kolabar the presence of a beautiful woman has anything to do with it. They simply shrug as he goes off to catch up with Badger. When he does accomplish this Badger looks to his left to acknowledge his presence.

"It has been quite awhile. I figured maybe I should stay close in case there is anything you think of you want updated on."

"Of course Illio I understand. That is quite thoughtful of you."

Illio makes out a sly smile from Badger. The conversation is not lost on Kanessa either even though she makes no visible sign one way or the other. The trio find Torman after about forty minutes. Among the dozens with him Badger recognizes a few such as Glite, Jolo, and Crale. A well uniformed rider next to him is most likely the Argonnes commander in Badger's mind. As they get close enough for Torman to recognize him he stops his mount. Those with him do the same. This is not lost on Killamon who is also present.

"He looks familair Torman I just can't place him or her. Who are they?"

Glite decides to enlighten Killamon.

"Sgt. Killamon you are looking at Badger. As for who is with him I have my suspicions on the answer to that."

At this point the new arrivals join Torman.

"I have someone for you to meet Torman. Say hello to Kanessa."

"Badger you are one surprise after another. I figured you were looking for her but I doubted that you would succeed. It is good that you are back among us. We have had to concede much. That is going to change though. This is Hixen who is commanding the Argonnes force that is here among us. The Covehi are no longer alone in this fight."

"That is good to hear. Now I have bad news to tell you. The orange eye is in the Mordagi hands."

"I can't beleive that. It was a safe place I sent them to. Cheelo had good men to protect it. They should not have found them."

"I'm sorry Torman but they did. After surveying the scene I accounted for all except Cheelo and Miranda."

"This means it will be impossible to launch anything against them without them having foreknowledge of it. In general terms they are back to being able to anticipate preemptively our plans."

Hixen shows disbelief as he listens.

"That legend you had with the orange eye was just a bunch of nonsense."

"You listen to me Hixen. I know you never believed the Covehi when it came to the eye but it does have properties like we always said. It is much more important then you know."

"Here is some advice to you Torman. Leave the folk tales behind. To fight alongside us it is necessary to learn true warfare."

Hixen at that point decides to move further up to consult with some of his men. Already Badger has formed some opinions of these new allies.

"Do most of the Argonnes share the trait of arrogance or is he an exception?"

"He is not that bad Badger believe me. I have spent a considerable time in his company. Their arrogance is well earned in the best trained, armed, and standing army outside the Mordagi. So do you think Miranda is dead or alive?"

"She is alive unless it can be proved otherwise. We need to have war council tonight there is still more that needs known."

"This evening after dinner than Badger."

17

Fluffy's Task

As mentioned in the land of the Sanders a new metal has been discovered. Fluffy with his apprentice Snackle has been hard at work locating Bormitian sites for future mining. During this work he has passed through the towns of Lawson's Reward, Cradles Hip, and Coffins Ridge. He has found a disturbing trend developing for which he has no explanation. At each of these villages he has made a stop at the local drinking establishment for medicinal purposes. That's what he likes to tell the barkeep anyway. That's when it happens. Now he is in the town of Five Fingers, and the trend persists. There are a few patrons scattered throughout the tavern minding their own business when a total stranger walks in. He is maybe half the size of Fluffy in comparison. In height probably even. When he first walks in he stops at the door as if looking for somebody. When he sees Fluffy sitting up at the bar he walks up next to him.

"Hey friend let me buy you a drink. I'm new here, and some local who says he has seen you before said your name is, get this, Fluffy. That's not true is it?"

The stranger being very unobservant misses seeing Fluffy tense up his hands holding the big mug containing his drink. It will prove to be a regret on his part. Especially when he taps him on the shoulder to continue the conversation.

"So come on, what is your real name?"

"My name is Fluffy you imbecile. It's a respectable name, and don't you forget it!"

The effectiveness of this statement won't be much because as it is being said the stranger is enduring a solid punch in his face. The result of course being a knockout in Fluffy's column. Besides the time needed for the broken nose to heal the stranger shall make a complete recovery. As the man lays on the floor Fluffy notices the barkeep start to bring over a bucket of water. A stern look makes the barkeep reconsider. It would likely be better to wake him up later. Fluffy goes back to drinking. The next person to enter the establishment is Snackle. He makes his way over to his mentor stepping over the motionless body on the floor.

"You can't be serious. Again."

"Yep."

"I just don't know why they like to mess with you big guy. It just doesn't make sense. Barkeep I'll have what he has."

As the two discuss their progress a new individual enters. His clothing is similiar to most everybody else's with a couple of noticeable differences. On the shoulders emblems of a tigers paw paired with a silver star on the breast of the person. A Tigerstar is accustomed to being noticed by the public so he is not surprised when things quiet down upon his entrance. What lawmen aren't though. Fluffy has taken note also of who has come in. The fact that it is Rippledutch himself Grand Tigerstar is highly unusual. He only handles matters that King Quid personally assigns him to. Rippledutch clean shaven with an air of professionalism proceeds over to the bar. As he does so Fluffy gives Snackle a questioning look. Snackle just shrugs his shoulders. Stopping right in front of Fluffy he verbally confronts him.

"You are Fluffy Flambay correct?"

"As a matter of fact I am. This doesn't have anything to do with this clown on the floor does it."

"Did he deserve it?"

"Every bit of it."

"Good. I have no concern about the clown you refer to. I have been dispatched by the king himself to find, locate, and deliver you to his audience. I must say you are not very hard to find. Along with two other Tigerstars you will come with me now. You should probably bring your apprentice also."

"In that case Rippledutch we are ready when you are."

With that statement Fluffy finds himself on the way to an audience with the King.

18

True Evil Revealed

The night has rightfully replaced the light of day as a important meeting takes place among the Alliance. Those in attendance are Badger, Torman, Kanessa, Glite, Killamon, Twistle, and Hixen. They all listen intently as Badger retales the encounter with Rolph Cramjelly.

"So there you go gentlemen. A red diamond also exists in the hands of the Mordagi which arrived at roughly the time all the trouble started. If we could get to it I beleive it's destruction would stop this war in it's tracks."

Hixen finds it to difficult to hold back his thoughts.

"I don't doubt this other diamond exists but it is also just a bunch of hocus pocus. The reality is the Mordagi has started a war that will only be stopped by a use of arms. Once we get on our side of the mountains the second they cross the line their end begins."

Glite decides to show support on that thought.

"I can't beleive they are under some type of control. It has no bearing anyway considering we still have to fight through them to get to it."

"Torman, you showed me a map just before I left. Have the Mordagi crossed the snake river?"

"No. What kind of crazy stunt are you thinking of now Badger?"

"With the Mordagi evidently preparing to advance into the Argonnes land now the bulk of their military has got to be involved in this. You said yourself outside the Mordagi the Argonnes are the next strongest military might there is. I follow the bank of the snake river until it bumps up against the Okoba swamp. There I cross making my way through the swamp with two goals in mind. Get Miranda back if she is still alive, and utterly destroying that red diamond."

"What about the swamp chameleons Badger? You figure they will just let you pass right through their land."

"That's true Glite but then again my sidearms I'm betting will penetrate their hide. If I'm wrong at least I know I've done everything I could. One way or another I will find Miranda dead or alive. I can't live not knowing."

There is quiet among the assembled for several minutes until Torman breaks it.

"My friend I care for Miranda to but you are setting out on a suicide mission. You forget something I think. You separate from us the wizard will detect you before you even make it out of the swamp even if the chameleons don't get you."

"He won't have to worry about that Torman. With my presence I will cloud the wizard from knowing what Badger is doing."

Among everybody their is a mixture of reactions. Hixen along with Glite show shocked expressions while the rest our taken by surprise with this statement. Badger is surprised to but quickly recovers his thoughts shaking his head.

"No way Kanessa. You need to stay here with Torman. I won't deny like Torman said this may well be a suicide mission. I am not going to get you killed to."

"Tell me something Badger, have you ever even been in the Drosch desert. To make a journey along the Sanders side of the snake river you will find it necessary to travel in it."

"You know I haven't Sgt. Killamon so just make your point."

Sgt. Killamon looks over at Torman as if looking for approval. Torman motions with a hand for Killamon to continue.

"Since Badger seems set on this scheme perhaps we should increase his odds of success. How many men do you wager would help ensure success Badger?"

"Thirty volunteers. Quite a bit of this operation will just depend on what happens as we go along."

Torman feeling that the council should come to an end for the night brings just that with his final words.

"I don't like this Badger but it needs to be tried. In two days we shall be out of the mountains, and inside Argonnes territory. You shall have your volunteers. While you are on this trek we shall with our allies fight the Mordagi with all the strength we can muster."

Everyone disperses with varying thoughts on what the future will bring. For now all will be content with a good nights rest.

19

Blacksheep Whims Included

In the royal palace of the Mordagi the Emperor himself conducts talks with Coffle as they travel down a quiet corridor.

"It sounds like everything is well in hand. I don't think the family could be safer. By the way where is my daughter?"

"She is down by the pond throwing rocks at the frogs sitting on the branches sticking out of the water. That will probably amuse her for a few hours."

"You know something Coffle. Everyday I wake up hoping somehow Shebith will be given wisdom instead of being such an idiot. We of course know this has not happened. At least my sons serve us well at least. If she was not family the answer to this problem would be so simple."

"Excuse me sire if this is out of place but perhaps her elimination would be more of a mercy for the family's well being."

"No Coffle. The sanctioned killing of a family member will never be allowed. No royal blood will spill unless in battle for the Mordagi empire."

"My apologies for such a poor suggestion."

"No apology necessary Coffle. I know you are just looking out in the best interests of the family after all that is your job."

"My only concern. I also wanted to ask if you are aware of Shebith's new request. It is another odd interest she is going to take up I fear."

"What is my daughter wanting to do now Coffle?"

"She is wanting to hold some kind of gladiatorial entertainment involving the mentally deficient."

"Go ahead with fulfilling her request. If it keeps her occupied, and out of other more important business of the empire."

It is at this point that footsteps are heard approaching the two. Coffle's instincts cause him to draw his sword. Just a few feet from them Sipian steps out from a side hallway. Coffle sheaths his weapon upon making this identification.

"Father the Hykolite lands are now ours."

"See there Coffle, can there be a better example of what we have been discussing. My sons at least produce results. That is promising news son."

"We have some pressing business to settle father. Miranda should be reaching Ohno any day now. You still have not made the decision on who gets her. Me or my brother."

"That is true Sipian I have not decided. You both want to make her your personal slave along with the other sisterhood when we find them. Miranda being the first I need to come up with a test to give both of you a chance. That is the question of the day though. What should it be?"

"If you will pardon me but perhaps a test of endurance sire."

"Interesting thought Coffle. Expand please."

"An obstacle course with a set of tasks."

"That is what is going to be done. You serve me well again Coffle. I shall have Warchuck set up this course for my sons. Listen well Sipian to what I have to say. You will go to pass this on to Cutnuts on how this will be decided. I expect him to leave the immediate warfront to his subordinates while he returns with you to settle this matter. Afterwards he will return to take back command of the front. You will take on a different assignment at that time. Understand?"

"Yes I do. I will leave in the morning if that is acceptable."

"It is."

Elsewhere in the empire at the prison camp Ohno new prisoners have arrived. Sparole is at the entrance of the camp to personally view these new arrivals. A column of riders slowly make their way to the entrance. Blackards both lead, and bring up the rear of the procession. Additional troops encircle a group of five prisoners whose hands are bound to the saddles which in turn are tethered to each other. Once they stop one of the Blackards prods his mount forward.

"Commander, these are the prisoners you have been given special word of."

"Yes Blackard. A very fine job done by all of you. I shall take custody now until the word comes down they want them in the capital. Evidently the Emperor has plans involving this group."

The prisoners are brought inside the gate to be handed over to troops of the camp. The prisoners are dismounted each led to separate locations. The men find themselves in small cells of three in a cell while Miranda is placed alone. Upon entering these confinements their bindings are removed.

The next day the prison accepts two additional prisoners. One male, one female both with healing injuries. They both go to a medical section of the facility. Their arrival not known by Miranda or the other detainees.

20

Alliances Build & A Rescue Is Launched

Fluffy's audience with the king has gone quite well. He has received knowledge of a war the Argonnes are about to be pulled into. Due to this the Argonnes have sent word to the Sanders they need to revive a long standing agreement known as the Armorers Deal. Under this agreement the Sanders who are the best weapons makers around will automatically supply the Argonnes with the newest weaponry anytime the Armorers Deal is invoked. The only time this cannot be invoked by the Argonnes is if they are the cause of the hostilities. In return the Argonnes maintain a strong flow of food, medicines, and certain other goods to the Sanders that can be difficult to find or grow in the Drosch desert. In times like these King Quid appoints a Weapons Master General. In simple terms this individual takes on the duties of overseeing the production lines at Horganpoe's Ring. The best in the field from across the land will receive notice of mandatory service which by their law cannot be refused. As in Fluffy's case this service will last as long as the Argonnes invoke the Armorers Deal. King Quid also has heard of this Bormitian, and questions how useful it will be.

"At this time I can state it is definitely stronger in every way then anything we have had before. I have also noted ample supplies in the territory. I do have to admit there are still some additional things I want to test about it. There is no doubt we will see dramatic upgrades in our weapons because of it though. That I'm certain of."

"The timing of your discovery of this new precious metal could not have come at a better time. Conduct your tests. Our new weapons should be forged with this. We need to start shipments to them as soon as possible. I have already sent word to them they can expect stronger weapons grade then what they have now."

Fluffy leaves the King knowing he has a big job ahead of him. One thought that occurs to him is that Snackle had better be ready for some hard work.

With the passing of two days the Covehi along with their escort have left the mountains to enter rolling plains which mark the begining of the Argonnes territory. Almost immediately they visually see several large camps with troops numbering in the thousands dotting the horizon. Hixen leads Torman, Badger, Kanessa, Killamon, and Twistle over to a particular tent which is the largest one in sight. As they near the front of the tent several troops step forward to take the reigns. When they enter there are numerous tables, maps, and about twenty five men all busy at various posts situated throughout the command center. Hixen with the others close behind goes directly to one of the larger tables in sight. The four men at that table sit up promptly followed with salutes. Hixen salutes back then sees to it proper introductions follow.

The next day Badger has prepared himself for the task ahead. His heart was warmed when Torman had said the number volunteering was much greater than the thirty needed. It was not the easiest thing to decide but the picks had been made. Badger recognized quite a few of the men such as Illio, Jolo, Trinit, even Twistle had decided to join this mission. Also in the mix were some not so familair to Badger such as Sgt. Killamon, Goosbe, Tolamar, Icepick, Knivenlaw and Itopoly. The remainder of this conglomerate of men he just had not had time yet to even learn their names. He was confident in one thing though which was they were all fighting men he would be able to depend on. As they move out Badger remembers a last minute discussion he had with Torman prior to the embarkation of the group. He had been informed that Ribble, Crale, and Kolabar were going to take out small units of their own into the mountains to conduct raids on the advancing Mordagi. Torman was hoping they could buy a little more time while the Argonnes finished all their buidup plans before the sides actually met. There was also one statement he made that Badger had not forgotten.

"I know that Hixen along with his other countrymen don't beleive the diamonds actually mean anything but I do. That means you may well have the best real chance to end this bloodshed."

Within a few days Badger along with his volunteers enter the Drosch desert. The trek so far has been uneventful which does not disappoint him. He has actually noticed in that time Illio being successful in gaining attention from Kanessa. On the second day in the Drosch Badger converses with Killamon, and Twistle on if they will likely come across any Sanders on the path they will be taking. Twistle more less decides to let Killamon talk as he just sits back on his saddle to listen.

"Except for going on the outskirts of Horganpoe's Ring not likely. It is out of their nature to venture out of the towns much. Traders are about the only ones who do on any regular basis."

"Perhaps we should stop in Horganpoe's Ring to just say hello. Show some courtesy about cutting across the land."

"That may not be a good idea. I'm not sure how hospitable they would be."

When they get to the point where the outline of Horganpoe's Ring is barely visible Badger decides on an action. With nightfall only about three hours away it seems like a good place to rest for the night. During that time Badger is able to talk Sgt. Killamon along with Sgt. Twistle into taking a ride into Horganpoe's Ring.

As they ride into the settlement Badger is impressed with how detailed the buildings of brick, and clay materials are. Quite a few are even up to four stories high. There is a abundance of food vendors along main travelways. Drinking establishments are present but widely scattered. Killamon tells Badger that this is their capitol. Upon receiving this knowledge Badger insists on a chance to see where the King resides.

As they proceed down a main roadway Twistle is the first to notice a checkpoint further up. Five Tigerstars seem to be conducting a search with the citizenry in their vicinity. Badger notices a side alley which he recommends they use. The other two agree deciding it was probably best to stay out of internal affairs of the Sanders. Unknown to them their presence in Horganpoe's Ring has actually been monitored the whole time by the Tigerstars. The appearance of a force, small as it is outside of town, should not be ignored. It was pure coincidence a Tigerstar returning from an assignment from Cradles Hip had observed them unnoticed. He had been quick to notify his superiors back in town. The notification of this situation made it all the way to Rippledutch. Rippledutch being of quick mind when it seemed appropriate promptly put forth a plan to find out what was up. At a number of locations men were positioned to set up checkpoints if these newcomers came their way. Each place left three options for the trio to take. First, they could make contact with the checkpoint. Second, there would be one obvious circumventing route or simply turn around. Rippledutch had expected the most likely result would be for the strangers to try the circumvention. So when they did just that as he watched from a window in a darkened room his smile was unstoppable. He could not help but remark to the other Tigerstar in the room on this.

"I love it when a plan comes together."

As the trio get halfway down the alley several large nets our thrown from roofs above them. All three of them are caught totally off guard. Among them Killamon is the only one to not be dismounted by this assault. Simultaneously mounted Tigerstars approach from both ends. Badger's mount goes down to one end of the alley while Twistle's goes to the opposite end. As they struggle to get their weapons unsheathed the Tigerstars are on them in seconds. Killamon is forcefully grabbed off his mount. Surprisingly he is able to deliver a kick to an opponents groin. Needless to say he falls rolling on the ground. Unfortunately the Tigerstars find no amusement in this as Killamon is clubbed from behind. The other two watch their friend go unconscious as they try to fend off the attack. It proves more then they can handle. Their weapons are seized from them as they surrender. They check on Killamon without interference. Badger checks vital signs then looks at Twistle.

"He should be okay. I bet when he comes around though he will have one hell of a headache."

Badger waits till he is erect again before he speaks again. As he does he makes sure to look into the eyes of as many as he can.

"You Sanders sure have a queer way of rolling out the welcome mat. What's this about?"

Among the Sanders lawmen a couple of them had small colored insignias on their uniforms. Three had them in green while another had it in blue. The one with blue directly confronted Badger now.

"I have orders to take you into custody. The orders come from Rippledutch himself."

"There is no way you could even know who we are. We have not done anything to deserve this treatment."

Twistle decides to break his silence at this time.

"What exactly does Rippledutch want anyway?"

"You will know in a minute. He is just around the corner in this building we are standing by. We will hold on to these weapons for now. I think you two can bring along your friend without help. Let's go."

With that Badger, and Twistle exchange a glance. They both prop up their still groggy friend between them as they are led around the corner into the building. Several Tigerstars stay outside the entrance as the majority take the prisoners up to a large room on the third floor. Besides a couple of chairs, and a relatively small table it is bare. Two Tigerstars post guard just outside the door as the rest go in with their detainees. On the far end stands an older man wearing the uniform of a Tigerstar but with a black cape, and a black insignia. He motions them to step over to the table as he does the same. He sits down gesturing them to sit opposite of him. Two lawmen take positions directly behind who is evidently their commander. At this point Killamon has started to come to but still needs to lean up against Badger. The two men help Killamon to the table to sit down. This accomplished they do the same. They quietly listen as the older man begins to talk.

"You have probably figured out that I have been watching you for hours now. I know you are not Sanders either. Why are you here?"

"We were peaceful Covehi passing through until now. Have you recently closed your borders to others or do you just have something up your ass?"

"Hold up Twistle. We just wanted to see the town that's all. It has not been our intention to offend you."

"I see. What is your name friend."

"Everybody calls me Badger. Twistle is my outspoken comrade while Killamon is the somewhat incapacitated one at this time. Do I get to know who you are.?"

"I am Rippledutch Grand Tigerstar appointed personally by King Quid himself. Once you saw the town how long before your force attacked us!"

Hearing that statement Killamon who has made a good recovery at this point looks over at Badger to make a point. Even though the timing could probably be better it seems to be lost on Killamon.

"Now if we just would have listened to me, and simply just kept going this would not have happened but did we 'no' of course not. Don't listen to Killamon. Now here we are."

"Are you done Killamon?"

"Yes I am Badger."

"Next time I will listen to your advice. For now let's try to resolve the immediate problem at hand."

"Be my guest."

"Rippledutch, the force you refer to is no threat to you I gaurantee. A force of Covehi are shortcutting through that segment of the Drosch to follow the Liber. Once we get to where the Liber borders the Okoba swamp we are going to cut through that to enter Mordagaiin territory where they won't expect it. We have a specific set of targets were going after."

"You are actually planning to go through the swamp?"

"That is exactly what we are going to do. We will succeed which in turn will end this bloody war between the Mordagi, and Covehi."

"A very interesting story Badger. We are aware of the war you speak of. In fact we have started rearming the Argonnes with newer weaponry. I will admit this is not how we usually treat newcomers to our land but with the tension near our borders one must be careful. If you were a threat to us I had to ensure capture with no escapes to tip our hand. Under the circumstances you are no longer prisoners. We also wish the Covehi well in this unfortunate situation thrust upon them. The Argonnes recently started suppling us with intelligience. This comes from King Quid himself."

"On behalf of our forces I am sorry for the apprehension we brought to you. By tomorrow afternoon we will be well on our way."

With that Rippledutch stands up to make a proclamation.

"May the fortunes favor you in this matter. I would also like to offer a docter to check Killamon if you would like."

Killamon having almost made a complete recovery at this point decides to answer that himself.

"My condition seems to have reversed itself Rippledutch, and since we are in a forgiving mode let the fellow who took the kick in the nuts know I said no hard feelings."

Badger along with his friends stand up. Badger extends his hand to Rippledutch. Rippledutch reciprocates the action as Badger says "I think that answers that. We'll be off now." A handshake is completed as Rippledutch nods his agreement to Badger's statement. Once leaving the building they find their mounts outside waiting for them. The Tigerstars with green insignias also were waiting outside. They returned all of the weapons seized during the disturbance.

The three very tired riders join their comrades back at camp around two in the morning. They first encounter Jolo, Trinit, and Goosbe who have received sentry duty for that night. As the sentries ask how the journey went the trio simply state it was a uneventful ride.

After a restful remainder of the night the raiding party seem to be reenergized for the mission at hand. After hearty breakfasts all the way around camp the time to move on is close at hand. The sun is shining brightly down on them as Badger roams the area seeking

Kanessa. It is a short search. To his expectation he finds her in Illio's company.

"Hey you two, how are things this morning?"

"Things seem to be well Badger. I was telling Kanessa a little bit about our raiding successes we had against the Mordagi."

The conversation is interrupted as a rider joins them. It is Twistle.

"Badger, we are about to have company. Looks like Rippledutch with about five associates. I was out talking with a couple of the perimeter sentries when I saw them coming."

"They probably just want to see us off. I doubt there is any trouble. Spread the word to totally leave them undisturbed."

"If that is what you want then you got it."

Only about fifteen minutes have elapsed when Badger finds the visitors riding up to him as he is walking amongst the inner camp.

"Welcome to the camp Rippledutch. Perhaps I could offer breakfast to you along with your friends."

"That is a pleasant offer, but no thanks. Looks like you are about to head out."

"We are about an hour away from doing so. You come out to check on our departure schedule?"

"Not really. I was hoping I had not missed you though. I have one of these men who wanted to meet you. He also has a request of you. Go ahead Fluffy."

At this introduction Fluffy dismounts while a smaller framed rider takes hold of his reigns. He pulls out a sword which Badger has to admit is quite impressive.

"I am in charge of the weapons production of the Sanders, and have developed weapons out of a new metal I have recently found in large quantities. In my hand is an example of what I am talking about. I heard of your presence along with some kind of plan to go into the Okoba swamp. Is this true?"

"You are well informed. My compliments."

"No compliments necessary. My position allows me certain priviledges that's all. I strongly beleive my weapons can penetrate the hide of the swamp chameleons. Due to this I would like to accompany you on this raid to see if I am correct on the effectiveness of them."

During this conversation about a dozen or so men have encircled those involved. Included among the closely listening group are Twistle, Killamon, Illio, and Jolo.

"You are actually sincere about this?"

"Completely Badger. Besides this weapon I have additional upgraded swords to arm about twenty more of your men."

"This seems like the perfect opportunity to find out if you are right Fluffy.

Badger takes a pause looking over at Killamon. Killamon understands the silent question nodding in agreement.

"You are welcome to join us."

"Great. I almost forgot my apprentice Snackle with also be with me."

"Okay. We will be moving out in about a half hour. Make sure you are ready."

With that Rippledutch offers one last good luck then departs with his remaining men. In two weeks time they find themselves on the bank of the Snake river with the edge of the Okoba swamp on the other side. Badger is in the front next to Illio, Kanessa, Killamon, and Jolo. He puts forth a decision as they begin to cross the Snake river.

"From here out Illio I want Kanessa to stay in the center of our band. I want a strong ring kept around her. Her presence will block the wizard not to mention her ability to sense dangers close by such as swamp chameleons. As far as command areas I will take charge of the lead, while Killamon you take the rear. Twistle, that leaves you the center."

21

Miranda's Situation Worsens

Back at camp Ohno Miranda is about to receive visitors. By now Sipian has made contact with his brother Cutnuts, and are currently riding through the gates of the prison camp. They have decided to have a closer look at the prize they will be competing for once they get back to Grandago. Before doing this they make an unannounced visit to the camp commander Sparole who is currently dining with a inhabitant that is seeking his favors. She has fair features with a slender body. As soon as the guards assigned to watch over his quarters realized who they were access to the room was completely unhampered. Cutnuts was the one to swing the door open to the dining room.

"Commander Sparole I assume. Sorry to disrupt your evening business shall I say but we have pressing business of our own you see. There is a prisoner we have reason to see. For the moment we are just passing through on our way to Grandago."

Sparole knowing better then showing disapproval about their entrance merely looks up showing mild interest.

"Well gentlemen I must admit this visit I was not expecting tonight. Nevertheless It is obvious for which prisoner you refer to. There is no question in regards to your full access rights here is there something specific I can assist you on?"

"Once myself, and my brother finish our visit we will rest for the night in your quarters please see to the arrangements."

"My quarters General . . ."

Sipian who had been visually assessing Sparole's tastes in the opposite gender detects a note of protest rearing it's head. The reaction is swift

"Do I detect displeasure in my brother's orders commander! It would be a terrible waste to have to report to Warchuck the need to question the loyalty of one such as yourself."

"I assure you Sipian there is no displeasure it would be my honor."

"That is much better. More appropriate of a Mordagi soldier to his superiors."

With that exchange over with the brother's leave to see the unsuspecting Miranda. Only a few minutes elapse by the time they walk to the building housing Miranda's cell. After making their way through quite a number of guards not to mention locked gates they find themselves looking at her. She is still in a cell by herself. She noticed the attention quickly, after all it is not often one has a visit from the heirs to the Mordagi throne. She stands defiantly opposite of them. Cutnuts speaks out an observation.

"She is indeed as attractive as we believed. Definitely a prize worth competing for wouldn't you agree Sipian?"

"Without argument. Her defiant streak will be amusing to break. Quite a bond mate brother."

The darker side of the conversation is not lost on Miranda as she listens. The disgust builds up to the point where she can't stay quiet.

"Neither one of you shall get any pleasure of any kind from me ever. Whatever your plans they will fail. You will not break me I swear an oath on that."

"She has quite a spirit doesn't she Cutnuts?"

"Impressive indeed. Listen well to this Miranda. Very soon one of us will be back. The one who does will become your bond mate. You will adhere fully to that authority regardless of what you think now. You will break. That we swear back."

Pleased with themselves the two retire for the night back to Sparole's quarters for a good night's rest.

22

Perils In The Swamp

Two days have passed with Badger's raiding party staying out of any problems. Badger feels their luck probably won't hold much longer. The day is still young when Kanessa passes word up to Badger she perceives a threat is close. Because of the overhead canopy of tree tops sunshine was illuminating only scattered patches of ground. The Covehi slow down to a crawl as they push forward. With the most intense alertness they can muster they scan all around them for the give away red eyes of swamp chameleons in disguise. Towards the front Jolo locates the first chameleon. He manages to fire his crossbow putting a bolt right between the eyes. A owl falls from it's perch. It only takes seconds for it to transform back to it's original self.

"Good shooting Jolo. Our presence must still be a secret to them. I think that was just a chance encounter."

"I hope so. It would not be helpful to our mission if we took on losses this early on."

Badger merely nods in acknowledgement. Not known to them unfortunately is that the following day they will come across a nesting area for the swamp chameleons. Due to the ground conditions it will be unavoidable. That day Kanessa is able to sense the danger about a half mile away. Badger takes a couple of minutes to discus the situation with Killamon, Twistle, and Illio. Fluffy also finds his way into the meeting.

"I figure I am not the only one who has noticed navigating through this land has gotten alot more difficult. I also have bad news. Kanessa senses problems up ahead. I know yesterday we only had one chameleon whom Jolo took care of but that by no means tells us what we are going to face today. We stick with the plan we have been using. Keep Kanessa protected well. As for you Fluffy, have all the new swords you brought with you made it into the hands of the men?"

"They sure have Badger. Since I did not have enough to give every single man one I did make sure all the men protecting Kanessa were armed with them first. It seemed logical you would want them armed as best as possible."

"Very good Fluffy. Thank you. This well could be the day we find out just how effective they are. As thick as the trees have gotten four abreast is about the most we can do. We are going to be spread out so just button up as best as you can. Fall back in gentlemen."

The men direct their mounts back to specific areas amongst the troops. It is late in the day with twilight developing. Already several stars have started their nightly appearance as Badger with his party find themselves in the midst of a nesting area. The wide marshlands has funneled them into a disjointed column as they continue on. The knowledge of this fact is of course not known to them since swamp chameleons hatch their young, which come from somewhat large eggs, just below the water line close to the banks. This particular nesting area they are traversing through currently has ten swamp chameleons overseeing it's protection. The sight of the Covehi so deep in the Okoba swamp at first cause the chameleons to disclaim their eyesight. They overcome their disbeleif in quick succession. Putting aside their reactions protecting the immediate area is the duty at hand. Besides they remind themselves, how can the Covehi defeat them anyway? Showing patience the denizens of the swamp wait till they have set up equal numbers to both sides of the enemy before beginning any action. They keep their eyes closed so as not to reveal themselves prematurely, while keeping their bulky forms under the waterline also. They wait till the intruders are lined up perfect for the attack.

The creatures work in unison as they all lumber out of the muck, and mire that helps make up the swamp itself. Along the column of riders the changes in the landscape do not go unnoticed. Several men are quick to yell warnings to those perhaps yet not aware of the situation. The melee quickly breaks into three basic sections of fighting. Badger in the front automatically charges at a gallup towards the first chameleon he sights. In the corner of his eye he sees that his left flank is being protected. Jolo instantly took up the position, and was maintaining it. Six others have emerged to become the front line. Five dismount handing off the reigns to the sixth fighter. Completing the quick hand off they advance on foot towards another chameleon that has shown itself. The creature facing off the two charging riders starts to put it's orb in the air when Badger fires four times. All four shots penetrate the thick hide. Both creature along with the orb fall lifeless to the ground.

In the mid section the fighting does not start out as well. Kanessa is tightly surrounded by fourteen riders. A total of four swamp chameleons have set up on the corners of this perimeter. Three fighters go down simultaneously. Illio, Thrake, and Canth realize how close they are to one. Wasting no time the trio advance on horseback. The chosen target is a mere thirty feet away. Amongst the rest Twistle has been thrown off his horse. Shaking off the fall he takes a stand within touching distance of Kanessa. An additional injury is sustained when on the outset Pichero's mount runs wild between two trees. The animal makes it through but Pichero lands to the ground with a broken right arm. Result is to find Pichero leaning up against a tree guarding his right arm. Another fighter takes a orb hit to the lower back. Death overtakes him in seconds.

The rear is able to organize the quickest. Facing two chameleons on the left with another on their right Killamon acts decisively.

"You three with me. Itopoly, take three yourself, engage to the left. Goosbe . . . Bolipe . . . keep the left over occupied till some of us free up to help. Go!"

The men obey the orders as one of the riders with Itopoly goes down from a poison orb hit. He takes a direct hit to the face.

Up front Badger has stopped his mount, swiveling his upper body back, and forth seeking a new target while still in his saddle. All the while Jolo still by his side. Jolo points to where five men have converged on a chameleon. The creature has taken a defensive stance by lowering it's bulky body close to the ground to protect it's soft underbelly. Doing so gives a relative feeling of safety to the being. For the first time in Statureo history that is about to change drastically. Tolamar is the first to strike. With a strong downward thrust his sword, being of course one of those made out of Bormitian, shows it's worth by cutting into the hide. A dark liquid quickly starts to ooze out from the wound. A squeel starts being emitted as the reality of it's situation hits home. The others inflict additional injuries in rapid succession. A very important victory for the good guys. During this success their associate left watching over the horses has met his demise from a orb hit to the chest. Witnessing this at close proximity Fluffy finds his apprentice trying to conceal himself under a horse without much luck.

"What the hell is this Snackle? This is outrageous. We are going to show backbone not cowardice now get out here!"

Snackle reluctantly does so. Fluffy has reacquired where the location of the last orb in their immediate area is. The metal ball makes a dive straight for him. To Snackle's amazement instead of trying to dodge it Fluffy takes his sword, and with one huge swing hits it full force. The orb careens away finding itself deeply embedded in a tree. It's controller trying to dislodge it while the protruding spikes show no sign of loosening their grip. Seeing the outcome of his action Fluffy lets the tip of his sword rest against the ground long enough to make a cocky stance. Snackle can only shake his head in response.

The trio, which Illio is a part of, has to their releif found the new swords are indeed effective. They also take down a swamp chameleon the same way.

In the rear Killamon scores a quick kill also. Unfortunately for Itopoly, whom has managed to lose his mount out from under him from a orb hit, sees another of his splinter group go down. At the same time Goosbe along with Bolipe have pinned down their quarry.

That's when it happens. Knivenlaw makes his move to irrevocably alter the course of the rescue mission. Even though his original mission was to kill Torman there was no doubt in his mind that to disrupt, not to mention seizing Kanessa, was far to important to pass up. Using the confusion of combat he moves right up next to her in the guise of protecting her. On the inside of his left palm he has a small leaf plant with a single thorn sticking out of it. This particular one in question has a substance which is not poisonous but does cause short term loss of consciuosness if injected. The affects are almost instant. This is evident as he appears to innocently reach out to touch Kanessa's right arm. As he does this action Kanessa feels a small stinging sensation in that arm. She looks down at her arm followed by a surprised look at Knivenlaw as she goes unconscious. Prepared for the fast reaction he is already grabbing her letting her fall across the front of his saddle. With his right hand free he fatally slashes with his sword cutting down two more of the party before they realize what is happening. At a height disadvantage Twistle makes a lunge to pull him off his mount to even the playing field but instead receives a strong boot to the face. Twistle is only disoriented for seconds but those seconds are all Knivenlaw needs to break from the pack.

As Knivenlaw gallups towards the front of the column weaving between obtrusive tree trunks Badger notices his approach.

"Hey Jolo, what's that fellas name? It kind of looks like there is something slung over his saddle."

"She must have gotten injured. They must be having more difficulty a little farther back."

As this is said the other five of the front line have engaged the remaining chameleon left in their sights. They hear the approaching horse but when they see the rider as being one of their own they pay it no mind. They encircle the enemy as it changes to the form of a black panther. For the creature it is an act of desperation. The hopes to defend with the great cat's claws is all it has. It manages to inflict one serious injury to the right arm of Larch as it is felled by a cascade of sword blows. During this combat Knivenlaw gallops right past them getting close enough to strike one down with his sword as he bursts past them. Badger just thirty feet away can't beleive his eyes as he witnesses the kill. With Jolo in tow they hastily begin pursuit.

"What the . . . son of a bitch . . . come on Jolo traitor in our midst."

Twistle being quick to grab a steed after the kick was also in pursuit keeping them just within his vision. Illio was the only other one able to break away to also pursue, and was right with Twistle.

From the mid section which by now was suffering serious attrition they pressed the fight nevertheless. They added another to their count as it squeeled in it's death throes.

In the rear the tenacity of Killamon, not to mention the rest of the men, help keep the remaining swamp chameleons they are dealing with off balance. They destroy the last two in the rear with no additional losses to their side. Seeing this is the case they proceed to help the battered men in the mid section who badly need reinforced. The last of the chameleons finally go down but do manage two inflict two more casualties.

Continuing through decaying trees, damp soil, the pursuit does not let up. Knivenlaw can make out the intensity showing in the eyes of his pursuers as he presses on. After a mile Badger decides on a slightly new approach to the matter. With his left hand still holding the reigns his right pulls a sidearm.

"Badger, are you crazy? You might hit Kanessa."

"I have decided that is not likely. I'm just going to slow him down."

A shot rings out. Knivenlaw feels a searing pain in his left leg. A bullet wound just inches above the knee joint. He grimaces in pain. Badger achieves his goal however. Knivenlaw tries to maintain a lead without success. Badger in one fluid motion, firearm already holstered, dives off his mount putting the full force of his body into Knivenlaw toppling him to the ground. The action rolls him over his opponent by just a couple of feet. Jolo goes to Kanessa's aid first. He grabs the reigns of Knivenlaw's horse, and gently prods it away from the fight. Then dismounting helps the still unconscious female to the ground maintaining a nervous eye on the fisticuff. Knivenlaw rolls away from Badger to stand up. As he does this the pain shoots in all directions of his leg. He leans up against a tree holding his wounded leg with his left hand. In the other a very long, sharp, knife. His sword still laying where it was knocked out of his hand as he was forcefully demounted. Badger stands straight looking at Knivenlaw with a hard gaze. Badger gives a brief questioning look over to Jolo.

"She has a strong pulse with good breathing."

"So what was your assignment Knivenlaw?"

"Questions. You have to take me first."

"Suicidal type huh? Have it your way."

Knivenlaw glances out to see the timely arrival of Twistle, and Illio. As they slow down in preparation to dismount Knivenlaw drops his knife then quickly reaches for a throwing dagger out of a pocket. Maintaining one motion he starts a throw in Illio's direction. Before he can finish the throw completely Badger reacts instictively drawing, and firing just as fast with a shot to the head. Knivenlaw falls straight back lifeless to the ground. Even so Illio finds the dagger strike a tree uncomfortably close for his liking.

"Thanks Badger."

"Anytime Illio."

The three walk over to Kanessa where Jolo is knelt over her. He expands on her condition.

"I found some leaves from a sleeper plant in his things. Kanessa has a pinprick on her arm where he must have injected it. She will be fine Badger. The effects should start wearing off in about half an hour."

"So this stuff isn't lethal."

"Just like Jolo said. It is a very short term thing. Her health will not be any different."

"We can be mighty thankful for that Illio. What are our losses guys?"

"I just know we lost men Badger. No point in speculating. When we go back we'll just get the head count than."

"Fair enough Twistle. When she has recovered we will do that."

Indeed within a half hour Kanessa is awake with quite a few questions. The group fill her in as they make their way back. Upon doing so the situation is assessed. They now number twenty-two with two of those seriously injured. The best news of course is that the Bormitian does work against the chameleons. They set back out on the journey after the proper burial detail is done. Two days later they find themselves riding out of the Okoba swamp. All across the horizon are rolling hills except to the far northwest. A mountain range is visible to the naked eye. Of course these are nothing in comparison to the Shastle mountain range. Regardless though they do exist.

"So this is the land of the Mordagi. Here is what we do now."

23

Two Giants Prepare

As the Shastle mountains level out into the plains of the Argonnes a large army awaits the arrival of a enemy just beyond the horizon. Most hold the beleif the Mordagi will not stop at the border. The Argonnes have prepared well for this eventuality. Troops, and material have set up defensive lines across the plains where the Mordagi could come out at. Cavalry, archers, foot soldiers, along with impressive catapults have amassed in these places. Two miles behind the most likely place they will try to breach is where Hixen the Argonnes commandant of the forces has set up the command base. The number of men under his command are almost equal to what he faces just inside the mountains. In the command tent Hixen presently conducts a meeting with several of his subordinates with Torman alongside him.

"Listen well to my words commander's. The placement of our forces has been done well. You have followed my instructions to the letter. This doesn't come to soon. The scouting parties sent out by Torman have all returned with news that the Mordagi are at the border area. Their reports are that they were able to inflict about fifty casualties on the enemies side compared to a loss of ten on their own side. The sheer strength of the enemy finally pushed them out. It seems that within the next couple of days they will make their intentions clear. At any moment our homeland may call upon us to perform our duty. So hear these orders again so we are clear. Any violation regardless of how small or massive on our territory will result in automatic declaration of war. We shall repel the enemy by all means necessary then fight them to their very doorstep. The Mordagi have a large army, but we shall not sway from our responsibilites. Make sure the men maintain a strong readiness. You are all excused except for Crape." All those assembled minus Crape, Hixen, and Torman file out of the tent. "I want to make sure you have the cavalry positioned like I have stated. There are two keys to our defense one of course being the quick reaction I expect from them. Have these orders been followed Crape?"

Crape answers in a confident voice as he stands there in a blue tunic with trousers of the same color sporting red singular stripes on the outside. A very decorative sword dangling from his right hip.

"Just as you ordered. They are in three clusters. There will be no place on the battlefield out of their reach if quick intervention is needed on their part."

"Very good. With them in place, our front line troops well entrenched, and the catapults in hidden points the Mordagi are in for a few surprises when they come at us."

Crape salutes Hixen asking if there is anything else. Hixen excuses him.

"Your plans are impressive. Where do you wish to have the Covehi in all this."

"I have been giving that careful thought Torman. The Covehi have been fighting practically nonstop now for months. You need time to rest up. Build your stamina."

A disturbed Torman halts Hixen before he can continue.

"Hold your tongue Hixen! We will not be held out of the fight."

"Stop the lecture. I knew that would be the response if I tried to put you in reserve. God knows you deserve it even though you are to bullheaded to admit it. I want your forces covering Trundle's Path."

The two men look over a map as Hixen points to a specific place. The map shows the mountain terrain as it forms into the plains. There is a swath of several miles for which the Argonnes anticipate the Mordagi will launch the attack. Everywhere else along this interface there are no smooth transitions except a very narrow one just north of the main area. This is of course Trundle's Path.

"What for? Only forces in a narrow column could use that. Put us in the fight."

"Torman, I need my forces concentrated where I have them. If they use it figuring we saw no danger in that direction it could expose my northern flank. Your troops are very good at close combat. If that would happen you can hold them at the tree line. We will set up a signal for you to give so I can send some reserves up to you if that happens. It may not sound important, but it is."

"Consider your northern flank protected. Assignment accepted."

Taking his left hand Hixen firmly places it on Torman's shoulders.

"Thank you my friend. That takes care of a important concern I had."

As Torman leaves the tent he thinks of some concerns of his own. He can only imagine the mass carnage most likely to occur when the two giant armies engage. It is hard to remember the simple life of farming he use to have. Memories of his family still burn strong within him though. These shall never be vanquished from him until death. This he has no doubt of. He also remembers Badger's force, and hopes they are doing well.

At the point where Badger's force entered the Mordagaiian territory the key personnel of the group are huddled in a meeting around a fire. As we take heed of this meeting Badger along with the rest of the attendees is listening to Twistle.

"You know I would rather be with you all the way on this. I feel like I'm abandoning you. Holding the injured back though with protection is the right thing to do."

"Well put Twistle. From the outset of this mission I have always planned to get as many back alive as possible. Every individual counts here. I want everyone to know this.

When you leave follow the swamp perimeter until it becomes the snake river again. Find a good place to hold up. If you don't see us after a week figure the worst, and commandeer some river transportation. Use that to make it back to safe territory."

Bolipe interjects his thoughts on the matter.

"Even though I will not be there I sure hope something happens that you can take advantage of. The Fortress is not a pleasant place. I hope you are able to get the answer to the question you seek."

Badger looks at Bolipe with a sober look knowing the toughest part is about to start.

"Listen up, except for those assigned to Twistle we leave in one hour."

The meeting breaks up as men prepare for the impending assault. Badger catches Fluffy on the side.

"You should feel good about the swords. You will be able to go back to report on their proven ability. You plan to accompany Twistle don't you?"

"I have decided I want to see you through this all the way regardless of how it turns out. You have greatly impressed me Badger. It is also inspiring to see how far all these men are willing to go for you. I'm with you sir. However, to help insure word of the swords effectiveness does get back Snackle will be accompanying Twistle. This of course does not mean I beleive we are going to fail, but one must have contingencies."

Badger can't help but find mild amusement with Fluffy's choice of words. A cheerful smile is given as he answers his friend.

"Contingencies. You would have made a good boy scout Fluffy. You share the motto."

"I hope that is a compliment Badger."

"It is Fluffy. Glad you are staying."

24

Too Many Targets

For two days Badger's entourage has shadowed one of the roads that goes to the Fortress. Several times only quick thinking and Kanessa's sense of danger kept their presence a continued secret. The last thing Badger wanted was their cover blown until absolutely necessary. Finally close enough to see the Fortress they find suitable protection among a area of huge boulders. To their surprise they also spy a huge camp just a couple of miles away from the fortress. From the view they can get Badger suspects it could well be a prison camp of sorts. During the daylight they stay well hidden. Darkness has fallen so Badger makes plans with the men.

"If I am right men we have two possible places they are holding Miranda in. Both look very well protected. The Fortresss tougher though because of it's naturally built in defenses. Not knowing which is the proper target means I want any ideas any of you have on launching strikes at both simultaneously."

"What about a diversionary hit to draw away some of the forces immediately before we commence what ever we decide on."

Jolo makes a point in response to Thrake's comment.

"With only 15 of us there is no one to spare to do that. Plus how could we draw away enough to really matter anyway?"

"Perhaps we should just choose one, and take our best shot."

"That's just it Goosbe. We choose wrong we won't have a second chance. We might as well split into two strike groups. I know I'm not alone in realizing this was a long shot. It's all the way to the end if necessary with Badger."

Illio takes a pause looking straight at Badger.

"Give the word Badger. It's not like they are going to tell us which one she is in."

"Perhaps that is not completely correct."

Illio along with Badger look at Killamon with an astonished look. Badger presses Killamon on his comment.

"Just what are you contemplating Killamon."

"The road we have been shadowing has had quite a bit of traffic. Suppose we pick out a high ranking Mordagi on his way to the camp or Fortress to take prisoner. Maybe we could get an answer to that question."

Badger is unable to hold back a half smile as he takes in Killamon's words. After a brief mental deliberation Badger places one hand on the shoulder of Illio as he answers.

"I wish there was a medal I could give you right now for excellent timing of ideas. What a great point you have. Persuasion can be a wonderful thing. Here is the plan. We will set up an ambush. We will give it one day to pick out a target we think might do the trick. If no luck there I will lead one group against the Fortress while Illio takes the rest of you to assault the camp. I started this in hopes of finding Miranda. If this means dying in the process so be it."

The rest of the night seems to never end. Each man making their final inner peace in their own way. All share the same assessment of how this is going to end.

As Badger sits alone next to a large boulder, Illio with Kanessa alongside, join him. They quietly sit down all the while Illio holding Kanessa in a warm embrace. Illio is the one to break the silence.

"Are you thinking of Miranda? I'm sorry Badger that was a stupid question. I mean how are you doing?"

"Actually many things have been floating around in my thoughts. Mostly Miranda but not all things. For example in the history of my world there was a place called the Alamo. It was a fight of a few men against a much larger enemy. A enemy led by a dictator. They had to know they were going to lose yet they stood their ground to the last man. I have always wondered what men in that kind of situation would think about. I think I know now."

Kanessa's soft voice is heard next.

"And what would that be Badger?"

"The only thing that matters is whether or not the individual in question has lived while holding a beleif to the fullest. A life is nothing if lived without meaning or true purpose. There is no way I can continue my life without knowing the fate of Miranda. She is my meaning in life. The soul mate that makes me complete."

The trio sit in silence for a few minutes until Badger talks some more.

"There is something important you two need to do for me. When we spring our trap tomorrow I give us a fifty fifty chance on successfully getting the information we need. If we are forced to assault both places I need to know somebody makes it out to let Torman, and the rest of the alliance know about it. If we don't find out what we need to know you will be the last ones. It is important you go find Twistle, accompany those men back."

"We will not leave you."

"Listen up Illio. Kanessa is to important to lose here. She has allowed, through her abilities, for us to get here. She has performed her purpose beautifully. It is time for us to take our shot. Succeed or fail the time is now. You two are in love so it is most fitting you be her escort out."

Illio realizes openly for the first time the truth in Badger's words. He indeed has fallen in love with Kanessa. He acknowledges the logic in what Badger has said with a sad nod.

25

Shebith In Custody

Gorrillo was a man who followed orders well. He was a soldier in his early thirties who was on his way up the ladder to being a general until he managed to anger Warchuck that is. His mistake was showing to much ambition at the wrong times. You see Warchuck was extremely comfortable in his command of the military which meant he watched those very carefully who might be wanting his job. At a party being hosted by Warchuck himself awhile back Gorrillo had ran his mouth on just that subject. In front of several listeners he said he would make a fine Supreme Commander. This of course made it to the ears of Warchuck before the conclusion of the night.

Needless to say Gorrillo found a reassignment order the next day. His position in the general's staff was being reallocated.

His new job was to take over the security detail for Shebith. Now this of course was an open secret among all the Mordagi military of just how much of a loathed assignment this was. There was not a soul alive who wanted the responsibility of watching over the Ogress. Who could blame them. She was a very fat, unattractive, sort of being. She had shoulder length brown hair, hanging ear lobes from the huge ear rings she wore, and had the table manners of a pig. In the words of the Emporer though "She is royal blood."

When Gorrillo found the man he was replacing he could not help but remember how quick he was in turning over the command to him. He managed to do it while he got his mount ready. Needless to say that was short. Gorrillo had a command of approximately fifty troops who were unfortunate enough like him to find themselves with this task also. It had only been three days since he took command, and right away Shebith got the urge to tour the prison camp Ohno. Most of the preparations for her upcoming gladiatorial games were in place, but she was going to look for possible additions to the event. Coffle had sent down approval for this trip. In addition a list was given to him of certain prisoners who were off limits to Shebith. It was a relatively small list which Shebith had already been made aware of from her father.

So now Gorrillo finds himself with a escort detail of thirty men just a couple miles from camp Ohno. Fifteen men, including him, in front of a horse led wagon with fifteen bringing up the rear. The ground slopes a bit with a few big rocks along the trail not to mention a scattering of trees.

They are but a short distance from a spot where the road bends when Badger's entourage attacks. Badger has reverted this time to using sword so that the noise from his sidearms not alarm potentially other Mordagi within earshot of such noise. In the rear of the column seven begin a savage attack into the Mordagi. In their charge from well concealed positions surprise is on their side. About half the men fire a salvo from their crossbows into the mounted men. Three Mordagi are taken down by bolts. Icepick even shows skill in throwing as a dagger of his embeds into the back of a Mordagi as well. Gorrillo, being in the lead, hears the commotion. His first reaction is turn around. Before even uttering a word the man closest to him along with another in the front fall off their mounts mortally wounded. Unlike the back the attackers in the front maintain their cover. Gorrillo shouts out orders to his men.

"Closest five to the wagon lead it to the camp quickly. Bring back assistance. The rest to the rear."

On his last word the driver of the wagon takes a crossbow shot to the chest causing him to promptly fall to the ground. As this happens Icepick has already tackled one enemy combatant out of his ride. Finishing the job he even mounts his prize to press the attack from the saddle. Quickly the losses are felt on both sides. Tolamar falls fending off three by himself. He does take one down with him. The fighters are successful in causing most of the Mordagi off their mounts. Nidgit is instrumental in helping even the odds. Being the shortest of the bunch he darts amongst the small battlefield loosening the straps to many of the saddles. After seeing the wagon lose it's driver Gorrillo points to one of his men after a growl of anger.

"You are suppose to be elite troops of the empire start acting the part. Get those reigns now."

Two more losses to the Mordagi in the front from crossbows cut the number down even more. Gorrillo sees his man get the reigns. Four of his men take up positions on all four corners of the wagon as it takes off. As it goes by him he hears Shebith hollering something. He is quick to answer.

"Shut up you fool. Just keep your ass in their."

Gorrillo with his remaining five men in the front turn their attention to the men in the rear. Only four are left of the fifteen he started with there. Their swords out they start a gallup into the mix. As they do so the crossbowmen in the front break from their cover to take out three more troops. Gorrillo sees them falling out of their mounts from the corners of his eyes. Cursing is heard under his breath as he starts to fear failure. For the freedom fighters they lose another. This time Goosbe goes down from a sword stab in his left side. As the wagon, with the remaining escort, go into a bend the sound of someone landing on the roof is heard. As they passed a very large stone Badger appeared making the successful jump. In total surprise he grabs the driver throwing him forward. There is a slight jolt as the horses with their wheeled burden runs over the man. Immediately the four Mordagi left find four riders in their path. Two receive arrows into their chests. The last two find themselves in close combat. Sword fighting from their mounts they are given no mercy as Badger watches his men triumph. Badger grabs hold of the reigns bringing it to a halt. He orders Itopoly to guard the new prisoner while the rest of them rush back to help at the ambush site. Itopoly quickly hands over his mount to Badger.

Upon entering the remaining fray Badger quickly notes the stats. The Mordagi have three left standing. He is also happy to note no more Covehi have fallen since Goosbe. Gorrillo watches his last two men fall. Gorrillo finds himself encircled. Even though outnumbered he holds his ground. He even manages a slashing injury to Canth in the leg. Badger walks his way amongst the men. They create a bigger circle as Badger stands before Gorrillo. They both stand with swords in fighting stances staring at each other. Sensing something different about his opponent Gorrillo speaks first. "Who in blazes are you? Definitely not Covehi. Where is your homeland?"

"Just a little place called earth."

"Badger! My wife told me about you after the encounter. She was part of the ambush that failed. La . . ."

"Laroa. I remember her. She is quite attractive if I remember right."

Gorrillo musters a smile with Badger's comment.

"I'm sure she will have quite a few engaging her company when they find out she has no husband anymore."

As Badger utters the last words to that statement his right hand has already grabbed a throwing star. In one quick motion he throws the star into the throat of a surprised Gorrillo expecting a sword thrust. Gorrillo manages to hold on to his sword with his right hand as he falls to the ground. He touches the impaled object with his other hand as he takes a last gasp of breath even while his eyes stare off into nothing.

Badger looks over to Killamon whom is part of the assembled men.

"We don't have time to waste. Take a couple of men with you right now, and get up to Itopoly. After we have hidden these bodies we will be right there. We will start the interrogation right away."

Killamon follows Badger's orders promptly by issuing commands to several men to accompany him.

After about a half hour Badger feels the scene has been cleared of all signs of any struggle or fight.

"Good work men. Let's get out of here so we can find out just who are prisoner is."

On rejoining Itopoly they find Shebith sitting on the ground next to one of the wheels of the wagon. Badger dismounts to take a closer look at the prisoner. He gives Itopoly along with the other men a questioning look. Killamon is the first to speak up.

"Meet Shebith. Emperor Gitch's daughter."

"Is that a fact, Killamon. In that case I feel sorry for Gitch."

The comment is not lost on Shebith who delivers a fiery response.

"You will all pay for this raid. My father will seek all of you out then punish severely till you plead for an end."

"So where are you headed Shebith?"

"I am on a important mission. Release me now before the entire Mordagi army shows up. You are nothing."

Badger takes one step closer then delivers a hard slap to Shebith's face.

"Wrong answer. You are going to answer my questions forth right or we use your large exterior for target practice. As large as you are I place bets my men don't miss at all. How many hits do you think you can take before it's over?"

Shebith looks at Badger with surprise which turns to fear. Beginning to tremble she starts talking."

"I'm on my way to detention center Ohno. I am looking for additions to my upcoming games."

The interrogation is interrupted as Illio steps up next to Badger. In his hand is a piece of paper with writing on it. Badger looks down at it as Illio points to a name included in a list. Just seeing the name brings a immediate feeling of hope, optimism, and confidence for success. Looking at Illio Badger questions him.

"Exactly where was that?"

"In her things."

Badger looks at Shebith contemplating his next set of questions. As he does so Miranda's perfect image runs through the back of his mind. Badger sees them riding horseback together along a beautiful stream. They stop, and the two lean up against each other. Miranda tells Badger her wish is that they defeat the Mordagi so she can start a life with him. He remembers the words he answered her with. Such simple words they were. Haunting words to his subconscious. My oath to you is that I shall protect, love, and provide the most splendid life I can with you. A kiss is started but Badger is brought back to the present by Illio.

". . . speed this up or what?"

"I am sorry Illio what did you say?"

"I said don't you think we should speed this up or what."

"Yes. Sorry about that. Where are the people on this list being kept Shebith? Are they at Ohno then?"

"There are many prisoners at Ohno. I suppose so. The list is made up of certain ones that I could not requisition. That's all I know about them."

Badger steps forward again.

"I swear that is all I know. Just end it."

Shebith breaks down into uncontrollable sobbing. Badger steps away to consult with Killamon, Illio, Jolo, and Fluffy.

"Looks like Ohno for sure. Let's hear your thoughts."

"We hit them tonight, and not at the front gate either since it is most likely the strongest side. If we are stealthy we can probably find a weak spot to exploit in our favor."

"Not bad thinking Killamon. Anyone else."

Jolo interjects a comment.

"To bad we can't just use Shebith as cover to enter the camp. If we could disguise ourselves as her escort we could take our time looking for Miranda. Maybe even get out without a fight."

"Unfortunately that grotesque mongrel will start squeeling the first chance she gets."

"If we could drug her somehow that might work Illio. Wait a minute guys. What was that stuff that Knivenlaw used on Kanessa? Think."

"wait a minute Badger. It's the sleeper plant but if she is knocked out that will look mighty suspicious."

"Is it possible to make just enough to put her in a state of mind we can control?"

"None of us could mix it just . . . what am I thinking. Kanessa might. The sisterhood was knowledgable on plants."

"Very good Jolo. Illio would you round up Kanessa please."

"Right away Badg."

The answer is promising when Kanessa is asked about such a ploy.

26

Titans Clash

It is midday on the plains of Argonnes. Scattered clouds with the warmth of the sun shining down. From the foot of the mountains they come. Perfect lines of Mordagi infantry. Shields reflecting back the sun. They step forward ever so slowly. Concentrations of mounted troops further back just waiting for orders.

On the other side Hixen watches with a set of binoculars. He has been waiting for the Mordagi to make a move. Now he will know if his defense plans will succeed or fail. He watches as his troops brace for the battle they are about to take part in. His crossbows set up so they have open field in front of them. The mounted troops strategically placed are heard as the men hold back on their reigns. The horses can sense the coming action, and show eagerness as they snort rearing their heads in all directions.

The Mordagi advance their men to just within range of crossbows. As Hixen watches he looks over to one of his lower ranking officers.

"That is a little bit surprising. The numbers are in their favor. I expected an all out assault on the front line."

Within minutes of their stop the Mordagi fire a volley from crossbows using the shields as protection. A shower of thousands of bolts cascade into the Argonness troops. All along the Argonness line a scattering of troops fall from this assault from the air. A second assault takes far less as the men are quicker to take proper cover. The Argonnes return the favor but have less affect due to the Mordagi having their shields much more meshed together. Hixen makes additional notes of the battlefield which cause him to send couriers to front line commanders.

In his company are two of his most trusted officer's Wallow, and Berlox.

"Look at the way the front has become overextended. He wants us to break forces away from our defensive positions to slaughter them."

"The minute we did those mounted troops are probably just itching to ride in huh Hixen."

"You got that right Wallow. It's not going to work though. They are going to come . . . What the hell is Lidilow think he is doing?"

In utter disbeleif Hixen sees one of his officers preparing to, what looks like, launch a charge.

"Wallow get down there, and releive that imbecile before we lose that entire section! He is also deranked. Berlox."

"Yes sir."

"Ride the lines. Reinforce among the troops we make them come to us. Only until they commit to a full assault do we pull back to the secondary line. Then we spring our surprises."

Berlox offers a crisp salute to his leader as he rides off to follow his orders.

To his great releif Hixen sees Wallow get there just as a contingent of his men break from their defensive positions. Wallow rides directly into the group triumphantly putting them back in place. Before the individual responsible for the action can utter a word Wallow has informed the individual responsible for the action of his loss of rank. He is left no choice but to fall into a position along those men just minutes before he was issuing orders to.

Behind the Mordagi lines the command left in charge by Cutnuts watches the war plans proceed. Among the group of a dozen or so one is heard commenting about the battle plan.

"so far just like we expected. Although for a minute it looked like some were actually going to break cover. It is time to commence the full frontal assault. See that the mounted force with the contingent of Blackards I set aside begin the move to Trundle's Path. Once we weaken them today tomorrow we hit them in the flank also."

All the men nod their heads in agreement. In a short time later on the battlefield the entire Mordagi line advances. The front infantry go to a run. The crossbow and archers hold back as the mounted charge forward at a gallup from the rear. The front of the Argonnes line digs in their heels. The open up with bolts, and arrows of their own. Mordagi fall yet they show no hesitation. Many fall but they engage their enemy. Once the sides are close enough swords are drawn from both sides.

From the vantage point of Hixen he knows he is close to unveiling his surprises. Two men standing close to him are two of his best archers. He has stationed them to shoot flaming arrows when the signal time comes to his catapults. Troops in the fight viciously swing their swords hammering at each other with all their might. Casualties are taken from a wide variety of blows. Stabs in the gut, severed limbs, crushed bone trodden on by hooves, and good old fashioned hand to hand. After a twenty minute fight at the line Hixen gives a signal for his forces to fall to the secondary line.

Hixen starts to ride down from his vantage point which is the signal to fall back. His subordinates all along the line see this, and promptly order the withdrawal. When Hixen views they have seen his signal he turns to return to his vantage point. The Mordagi had begun to push his forces back anyway so the move should not make the Mordagi suspicious. He is correct. They continue onward in pursuit of their quarry. After about two hundred feet two arrows are seen flying through the air. The Argonnes reform lines of defense as from unveiled positions huge catapults begin launching huge rocks, and some flaming ones to. This ammunition lands right in the midst of the Mordagi troops. Even though battle hardened a large portion show surprise. Several huge swaths of destruction show in their ranks. Many of the mounted are flung from their horses. A dozen or so are even trampled or break their backs from the fall. The battle line seems to stabilize for the time being. The right flank seems to falter a bit so Hixen sends in part of his cavalry troops to halt the enemy's advance. The continued assault from the catapults do not ease. Finally the Mordagi commander sounds a recall to his troops. The losses to his side was more then he expected but he shows no sign of defeat. He has no reason to since severe losses were also suffered to the Argonnes. The next assault with the attack from the flank should open their lines up like a gutted fish. When that happens their fortifications, and other defenses will do them no good.

27

Search At Ohno

The sun has pushed back the early morning clouds as a escort delivers Shebith to the gates of Ohno. Guards at the gates halt the group as they make their way up. In their Mordagi garb Badger, accompanied by Killamon, brush up against the guards with their mounts. Badger speaks with a guttural tone.

"What is this? Can't you tell the royal seal when you see it. The carriage has royal blood inside."

The guards stand their ground withholding any emotion as they reply.

"Listen here. Identification is required. We have to see who's there before you go by us."

Badger gives a glance to Killamon who pulls back on his reigns a bit. Killamon then gets down from his saddle. He taps twice on the conveyance.

"Shebith, you need to address the guards."

Shebith exits to stand by Killamon. She simply looks at them, and gives them a flat answer.

"I am here on business of the state. Remove yourselves from my path."

The recognition is immediate the reaction is just as immediate. The most senior man answers her.

"As you wish. Please proceed with our compliments."

Shebith reenters her domain. Killamon remounts placing himself back next to Badger. They then proceed in all the while Kanessa closely monitoring the vital signs of Shebith from inside the carriage. The size of the camp has finally stabilized. The number of prisoners rest at 653. Sparole maintains a well disciplined force of 1000 guards along with a contingent of 20 Blackards. Their procession finds a nice quiet place to place their mounts. Badger walks over to the door, and taps on it. The door opens partly enough so he can see Kanessa.

"How is it going Kanessa? She going to stay the way we want her to."

"The doses I gave her should keep her compliant. Just remember one thing. If we stay into the night I can't guarantee anything."

"Gotcha. By nightfall we will get ourselves out of here."

The discussion is interrupted when Jolo catches Badger's attention with a hand motion. Badger notices Sparole with five men approaching. He shuts the door as if not seeing their approach. A loud voice rings out as Sparole reaches the men.

"It has come to my attention I have an honored guest. May I offer a personal tour . . ."

Badger steps in front of him.

"Keep your distance! You don't just walk up to a member of the royal family like you are omnipotent. She will decide who she wants to see, and when she seeks your audience."

Sparole's men are loyal to their camp commander so all five partially draw swords to show their disrespect to the newcomers. This does not go unnoticed by Badger's men who take on defiant stances. Killamon draws his own sword as he stands next to Badger. The disturbance is interrupted when Shebith exits her conveyance to intercede.

"What is the problem? Why do I see my personal guards being confronted by your men. You are Sparole the commandant here correct."

"Yes your highness. I was here to offer you a personal tour when your escort took offense to it."

"When I need anything I will let you know. I will conduct my business with my own men."

A agitated Sparole knows his best action is to withdraw.

"Of course. I give you full compliments plus anything you may need."

With that he, along with his men, depart.

Badger waits till they are well out of sight before he speaks to Shebith then his men.

"You are doing very well Shebith. What you want to do now is inspect holding cells. The first ones you want to start with is the high value prisoners first. If they remind you those prisoners are off limits say you understand that but you still wish to inspect them. Everyone else we just escort. I know we are not going to like what we see, but we have one goal. We find Miranda. The moment we do we have to quickly secure the area around her. Silence all the guards within earshot. No getting sloppy. We will have one chance at this. Part of you will get back to the mounts, and carriage. With as little fanfare as possible get back as close to us as you can. We make a break to the horses, and ride like hell getting out of here. If they reinforce the gate to quick we will use Shebith as a shield. Surely they won't risk royal blood. Everybody got it."

All the men nod their heads in agreement.

It is early in the afternoon as the inspection begins. As they find a wooden barracks which they have been directed to Badger makes careful notice of the compliment of outside guards. It is almost triple any other barracks in the camp. Badger's heart goes frigid as he calculates in his mind the true odds of success. Even so, he knows he can depend on these men to the end. He also knows he could not continue on not knowing Miranda's fate. They enter a door into a rather generous reception area. At a rather large desk near another opening a mid ranking Mordagi sits at it. He looks up at them with a disciplined look. To the side of him in a adjoining room maybe a dozen or so men partake in some kind of card game. In close reach of these men various swords, crossbows, even menacing maces. Shebith walks over to the officer. The officer stands up to address Shebith.

"Your highness."

"It is my understanding the more important prisoners are kept here?"

"That is correct."

"I am going to take a look around."

The Mordagi trooper stands in front of her for a few seconds then stands aside as Shebith, and her escort walks past him. They enter the corridors of prison cells. Only about half of these hold any prisoners. Those cells that do are scattered throughout the facility. Badger, along with Killamon, stay very close to Shebith as they walk through the cells. Shebith takes her time given occasionally longer looks at some. They walk through about half the facility when they come across the first prisoner Badger recognizes. The rest of the men do to, but remain very quiet. He taps Shebith on the shoulder. She stops to give him a glance. Badger whispers they want to have words with the prisoner. The black man sits up from a bed looking at them. He offers a puzzled look. Since there are no Mordagi troops within earshot Badger speaks.

"Cheelo. It is good to still see you alive."

Cheelo can't help himself from interrupting.

"What are you doing here. I mean all of you. With her even?"

"Listen Cheelo. Where is Miranda? She is here right."

"I'm sorry Badger. I just don't know. Since we were brought here I haven't seen her since."

Badger feels the fear of the unknown creep into his mind. He clenches his fists. Killamon puts his right hand on Badger's left shoulder.

"Badg listen, we haven't searched it all yet. She could be just around the corner."

Badger nods in agreement. He slowly unclenches his fists.

"Your right Killamon. I'm sorry. Listen Cheelo. When we have found her we will not leave you behind I promise."

Cheelo just gives a solemn look to the men.

The group moves on to continue the search. A short time later they come across Zandra. She is able to pass on some vital information to them.

"Cutnuts came, and was forcefully making her accompany his entourage. As they passed through here I heard him say she would be a very good bride once he broke her. I beleive he was taking her to the capital."

Badger turns to his men making a quick address.

"Our time here is over. We will get Zandra, and Cheelo out with us. I am not going to sugarcoat this. Some of us probably won't make it out, but we all accepted this when we came. I just want to thank you all one more time for everything."

Badger looks at Illio next as he gives instructions.

"Take five men with you. Get the horses, and carriage ready as close to us as you can."

"As soon as you get outside we will be ready to help cover your exit."

"I am giving you about twenty minutes then it is do or die understand."

Illio quickly singles out five men who leave with him. Once the time has elapsed the rest move into action. Badger instructs Shebith to call for a guard. She does. In a matter of just a couple minutes two guards come into sight along the narrow passage. They stand before Shebith questioning what she wants. As they do both men find themselves muted as sword thrusts into their chests from behind end their lives suddenly. A search of their persons finds one with a key to the cells of that particular area. Zandra is released.

"What about the other prisoners in this place?"

"I hate to leave anyone here, but we are here for a specific mission. We have to move fast. The only two going with us is going to be you, and Cheelo."

Zandra prepares to protest, but Jolo intercedes.

"We don't have the luxury of time Zandra. Only a few of us will probably make it. Any extra time spent here would most likely doom us all."

Badger leads the way back. Along the way true to his word they free Cheelo who, along with Zandra, stay as far back as they can. Four more times a total of five guards suffer the same fate as their predecessors. Then they reach the entrance where the dozen or so guards were at. They hold up at the doorway just out of sight. Badger gathers everybody quietly with a plan to deal with this last obstacle to the outside.

The mid level Mordagaiian officer is still sitting at his desk as Shebith, with the escort of Badger's men, return through the entrance of the cell blocks. He shows mild entrance as they pass his desk. As one of the men appear to be in the motion to open the door Cheelo accompanied by Zandra charge into the room. Before the officer at the desk can react he takes a sword stab in between his shoulder blades that penetrates to the other side. Instantaneously Badger adds to the confusion.

"Quick! Get Shebith to the wall. Create a shield. Prisoners loose."

As he utters the words the guards from the adjoining room fall over themselves as they grab the closest hand weapons they can to confront the jailbreak. None give it a second thought as they rush forward, while Shebith's escort stays behind them to instictively protect the royal blood. Standing side by side in the entranceway the two would be escapees make a stand. They are pressed hard, and the entranceway is small enough they are able to keep from being flanked. Once they all have their backs to Badger all pretense is dropped. Most go down before they are aware of the reality of the situation. Only the last five Mordagi go down with that knowledge. Badger does lose one man in the melee.

By this time Illio has managed to bring up the horses, and carriage within a short run of the prisoner holding facility. No notice has been given to their movement by any of the enemy. Illio does note a Blackard approaching the entrance. He feels his muscles tense but knows he is not in a position to do anything. Everyone is mounted anticipating action any minute.

That's when all hell breaks loose. Just as the assasin places his hand on the door to open it he is knocked to the ground as it is flung open. After opening the door with as much force as he could Killamon sees the man on the ground directly in front of him. He wastes no time in dispatching him by a quick sword thrust into his ribcage. Killamon ignores the look of total surprise by the Blackard.

Badger is second out as the rest stream out behind him. Keeping Shebith in the middle they scramble to the horses. Badger throws a grenade to a batch of Mordagi who are directly in their path the second he clears the door. His successful toss blows a wide gap in the closest Mordagi compliment. Almost a dozen are dead or dying on the ground as the band make their way to their mounts. Even though the Mordagi are taken by surprise the disciplined troops are quick to react. As the group rapidly get saddled up Illio along with the others mounted give support fire from their crossbows. Several more Mordagi go down. As Badger prepares to mount Kanessa opens the door of the carraige to hand him his shotgun, and a gunbelt with a sidearm holstered. For a second Badger thinks she intends to join the fight, but Illio sees to that. He leans down from his mount pushing her back in.

"Stay in there where it's safer!" With everyone now on horseback, and Shebith placed in the wagon the charge through the gauntlet starts. From the sides Badger sights riders approaching having heard the alarm. Also as they make a break for the front gate still just out of sight several Mordagi let loose volleys at them at several points along the way. The sudden flurry of activity has been noticed by Sparole as he takes a look out a window. The center of the activity is on the opposite side of camp. He quickly grabs his sword along with a shield within arm's reach as he exits to the outside.

By the time Badger's entourage reaches the point where the gate is clearly in view the group has been reduced to Badger, Illio, Killamon, Jolo, Fluffy, Icepick, Nidgit, Itopoly, Cheelo, Zandra, and Kanessa. As they get in close proximity Badger sees a strong Mordagi force standing in their way. He pulls hard on his reigns causing his horse to kick up it's front legs in protest. The rest follow suit as Badger grabs Shebith from the carriage. Putting his sidearm to her head a warning is given. As he gives it Kanessa makes her way to Illio's side. He quickly extends his hand to pull her up behind him.

"Listen well. Keep your distance or the Emporer loses a daughter. Clear the way, and I will let her go on the other side."

Badger watches as a Blackard makes a step forward. Badger shows no hesitation as he fires two shots into the target. The Blackard drops immediately to the ground stone cold dead. The Mordagi troops hold their positions. Sparole has made his way to the stalemate. From a tower overlooking the gate he addresses Badger.

"Do you really think we care about her? By being a casualty of battle you will do us all a favor. You are not getting out alive."

Killamon leans over to Badger. Badger listens to his words as he speaks very quietly.

"I hate to say it, but I don't think she will be much of a shield after all. They are way to confident. I think they truly are hoping she doesn't survive."

Badger stares straight into Sparole's eyes. There is no flinching or nervousness at all. Badger answers quietly back to Killamon.

"Damn. Your right. We charge the gate on the count of three. Good luck everybody."

Sparole starts to make a hand gesture to his men as he begins to smile when Badger makes a move. He takes a hand grenade tossing it into the crowded Mordagi at the entrance. Several others amongst the group let loose several crossbow shots. Two almost hit Sparole as one man next to him is not so lucky.

Again a gap is created in the Mordagi ranks. The freedom fighters plunge full force into the breach. Badger's party makes it through, but not without two additional losses. Icepick is thrown from his mount when it takes fatal injuries. Icepick never even has a chance to get up before he is swarmed by sword slashing Mordagi. Badger also notes Cheelo being tackled off his mount by a Blackard. The Blackard snaps Cheelo's neck as his body hits the ground. Sparole quickly organizes search parties. All return empty handed.

28

Battlefield Shift

In the land of the Mordagi Emporer Gitch walks with two of his most trusted advisers. It is a pleasant evening as they walk along a sandy shore with just a hint of moonlight. The men listen closely to their leader.

"The time has come for the killing stroke on the Argonnes. Are you ready to carry out that strike Warchuck?"

"The special task force is ready. They have completed the detailed training of the mission."

"This is splendid my friends. The message has been sent for the withdrawl. While the Covehi, and their friends the Argonnes foolishly think they are pushing us back we will position ourselves for the kill. Sipian will join the forces to take charge of that. I saw to it that while they were both here I let them in on the master plan. Cutnuts was going to be the one to assume command there, but we all know he has some work to do here now. He has returned to Ohno to take possesion of his prize. He will be back any day now."

"You will excuse me your highness for mentioning a concern I have."

"Please Coffle. Proceed."

"From the events that transpired just a couple of days ago have you agreed to my more thorough security plans for Grandago. It seems most likely that Badger will find his way here next. One last thing. I know

Cutnuts is extremely capable of performing his plans. However, does he plan to let me assign some more men to his quarters at least until we are confident she has submitted completely to his authority?"

Gitch looks Coffle in the eyes as he offers a big grin. Patting him on his back as he answers.

"Your beleif coincides with Hob about Badger's intentions. Badger will only succeed in walking into our hands. We will pick him up easy enough. He will never make it into Grandago on his own. Continue to make sure no one enters without the proper paperwork. The only real disappointment out of the whole thing is that my daughter managed through it unscathed. When I first heard about it I had certain hopes on her status."

"You were not alone I must admit."

"Even though I do not think Cutnuts will need it, if it will make you feel better Coffle you assign any extra personnel you deem proper."

"Thank you my lord."

With that the meeting is adjourned. In the distance silouettes of dozens upon dozens of ships can be seen in the moonlight.

Back at the the Argonean front this is when the second day of fighting is about to begin. The Mordagi not discouraged by the previous days fight feel confident of a victory. The sun has started to rise when Sipian with a contingent of personal guard arrive. They are followed by the force sent to Trundles Path. Livencurse, the general placed in charge by Cutnuts during his absence, listens with apparent dissatisfaction. His experience in the military, and longevity like Warchuck was his best choice. Livencurse was one of the extremely few who could openly show disagreement with a member of the royal blood.

Livencurse Japney was a very strong man with a thick respectable beard. It was as black as night like his hair. Probably 6'1 would be fair to say. He had one very remarkable feature that caused him to stand out. His left eye was blue, but his right eye was a sort of hazel.

"Withdrawl. Why the hell do you want to do that. There is no way they can withstand another assault. Hitting their flank at the same time would have clinched it."

"Now hold on Livencurse. My father wants to pull them into our territory to finish this army off. There are things in motion you are unaware of. As of this minute I take over this command. These are your orders General."

Livencurse is then shown a map showing the series of withdrawls, stands, withdrawls he is to execute. As he looks it over there are those who would swear he breathed fire as he pounded his fists into the closest tree. This was short lived though as his self discipline took back control. He dutifully looked at Sipian showing acceptance of the orders.

By midday Hixen is at a loss to explain why the Mordagi have not continued the assault. Late in the day he decides to send Wallow out with a scouting force of 30. They return late in the evening. When they do Hixen is sitting at a table in his personal quarters. He hears Wallow calling him out as he rides up. He exits to see Wallow dismounting.

"Your plans worked Hixen. They are withdrawing back to their side. We spied long columns going back. The only thing holding up was some of the mounted troops. My bet is as a simple rear guard action. You know. Protect the retreating columns."

"Are you sure? Besides some mounted being held back everything else was on the move."

"Yes. We did."

"It seems to good. Everything was going in their favor. Put the word out Wallow. Tomorrow at sunrise I will set out with all the mounted troops we have. We will hit their rear guard as quickly as possible. You will follow up with the rest of our forces. Have Berlox personally contact the Covehi to leave Trundles Path. They will want to join in."

"So we are going to pursue them after all?"

"The King was specific about what to do if they crossed the line. We shall pursue all the way to Gitch's front door."

Wallow gives a nod of understanding. Hixen goes into his tent to catch a few hours of sleep. For tomorrow the time to chase down the enemy will begin.

29

Road To Grandago

The remnants of Badger's raiding party has managed to meet back up with Twistle. The rejoining is a mix of emotions for all those involved. Out of the fifteen Badger left with for the raid Twistle counts only six returning along with no evidence of Miranda. He does receive a surprise seeing Zandra with them. Although Badger is very disheartened at the outcome thus far he is glad to see Twistle was able to find a safe place to wait for them. Plus the two with broken arms, which are splinted snugly to their sides, seem to be in better spirits since he last saw them. After they have had a chance to sit down, and eat some fresh meat cooked over a spit Badger fills in Twistle on what all happened.

"so when are we going to leave for Grandago?"

"We aren't Twistle. Everyone has fulfilled what I requested. We conducted the search into Ohno. I am going to finish the last leg of this journey on my own."

Twistle looks down shaking his head muttering as he does so.

"No. No. No. What are you thinking?"

Twistle then looks back up at Badger.

"So you just plan on going into Grandago all by yourself. You don't have a chance it is suicide."

"It is not any different then the raid on Ohno."

"Wrong Badger. You went into that with us. You gave yourself a chance. It might not have been much of a chance but a chance none the less."

Badger smiles as he listens to Twistle.

"Twistle, I could not have had better men then I have had come with me on this mission. We lost many who I will never forget. Enough is enough though. This is a personal matter I must finish alone now. Up to this point there was some military value to this mission also. There really isn't any anymore. I am ordering the rest of you to start heading back first thing in the morning. Find a good place to cross the snake river then back through the Drosch to Torman. Give him my best regards when you rejoin him please."

"Why end it this way for you Badger."

"Let me put it this way for you. I would rather live a short life I could be proud of instead of a long life with nothing to look back at. If that is what happens then so be it."

The news spreads amongst the group. All solemnly accept the instructions. That evening as Badger stands along the snake river he is joined by Illio with Kanessa by his side. They talk of their times, and experiences. Badger tells them he feels they will have a tremendous life together. They will have children that will make them proud. Their conversation goes quite late. All those in the party have gone to sleep except one lookout. Badger decides to leave while they slumber. He informs the two he is going to depart. Illio gives him a handshake, and a pat on the back. He tries one more time to get Badger to agree to have him accompany, but Badger holds the line. Kanessa with tears in her eyes gives Badger a kiss, and warm embrace. Badger slowly let's go.

"I hope you find her. I wish you all the success in the world Badger."

"Thank you Kanessa. For everything you did for me. You saved my life. Take care of Illio for me. He's a good man."

With that Badger walks to his horse. As he rides out of camp quietly he sees Itopoly who is on lookout. He waves him a farewell as he disappears from sight. The next morning when the camp awakens they start their journey back minus Badger. A rear guard action of 300 Mordagi horsemen have stayed back at the first mountain pass. They watch impassively as a leading element of around 500 Argonnes riders head straight for the pass. The pass has a width for about 100 horses abreast. The Mordagi block the pass with a wall of riders two deep. The remaining 100 dismount evenly distributing themselves on both sides amongst rock crevices, and other cover. As Hixen leads his men into what becomes a funnel which is the pass he sees the Mordagi. He throws up his arm to halt his forces. wallow rides up next to him.

"Sword arms ready men. Wallow, quite a impressive formation on their part."

"Yes sir. Quite impressive."

"Let's go break it up. Charge!"

With swords held high the Argonnes fling themselves into the Mordagi. The fighting is savage as the participants slash, and stab into their opponents. Men are dismounted, and pummeled into the ground. The Argonnes find themselves under attack from the sides as well. The Argonnes in the rear of the action begin assaults on the sides to clear out the snipers. It is a difficult, and slow process as they do so on foot. The entire skirmish goes several hours. Hixen is left with 100 riders out of the lead element. The Mordagi went to the last man. Hixen discusses the situation with Wallow.

"They really hurt us today. It was a mistake to let the forces get so spread out. While we are going through the mountains we shall keep everything tight from here on."

Badger wearing Mordagi clothing, and weapons out of view manages well traveling to Grandago. He encounters light contact with the traveling public. Those he does don't give him any notice. He does pass a couple small Mordagi patrols without incident. In all the time to arrive to Grandago is just under ten days. Badger has got just over halfway when he comes across a wagon along the pathway he is on. As he stops next to it he realizes the wagon has bars, and holds several captives. A man somewhat pudgy with an air of arrogance is feeding his horse team. The man watches Badger closely as he rides up. Badger decides to keep up the charade as a simple traveler to learn what he can on this unusual circumstance.

"Hello there. Are you heading to Grandago also?"

Still showing suspicion the man answers cautiously.

"Yes. I have a delivery to the gladiatorial games."

"Gladiatorial games you say? What lot is being put in those?"

"The mentally challenged. Shebith's idea. Say, have you been away from the capitol for awhile?"

The pudgy man shows more suspicion in his mannerisms as Badger speaks.

"As a matter of fact it has been awhile since I have been in the capitol."

A thought crosses Badger's mind, and he decides to act on it. As the man starts to ask Badger from what village he is from he receives a blow to the face that knocks him to the ground. Bleeding from his left nostril he finds himself being picked up, and being thrown against a tree.

"You piece of trash. The level of contemptuous swine I have seen in my lifetime continues to amaze me. How much profit will you get from this poor lot? They don't even have the slightest idea what their future holds do they!"

The stranger has turned to face Badger.

"Yea. They think it is a sightseeing trip to the capitol. Less trouble that way."

Badger is incensed by the callous remark, and delivers several blows to the man. The man tries to steady himself against the tree as he delivers his last words.

"It will be a hefty payment."

"Not for you."

Badger impales a very impressive dagger into the pudgy man right in the aorta cavity. After searching the man's clothing he finds documents relating to his purpose to the city. Badger feels his odds of success have gone up now that he has a cover to enter the city under. He admits it is not a huge swing in his favor, but something is better then nothing. He finds a good concealed place off the beaten trail to bury the body. Dark is about to set in so he sets camp for the night.

Meanwhile in the Shastle mountains the Argonnes army moves through in a massive cohesive force. Hixen has accepted the slower moving force the best way to proceed. Unknown to Hixen after all of his forces have moved past the previous battle that the site of the battle is having visitors. All the Argonnes casualties had been cleared. However, in the interest of time not all the Mordagi casualties were cleared. Many of those in the cliffsides were left behind. Also in the dusk five figures are seen walking amongst the remains. This is the first time this race has ever touched Staturian soil.

They are called the Dentolia. On their homeworld they are the only intelligent race. They live in a desert environment. The Dentolia are a golden skinned race, skin like leather with a single braid of black hair shooting out the back of the scalp. Another noticable trait for them are their four extremely sharp fangs spaced evenly among their regular teeth. To put it plainly the Dentolia are a race of bloodsuckers. The only thing their bodies can intake is blood. On their world they live off the blood of grown animal herds. Through a bizarre twist of fate they have found Statureo. On their world they are the only intelligent race. Their are no humanoid lifeforms but their own. Through this twist of fate they have found the taste of human blood much more better then anything they have ever had before. For now their little exploratory trip shall remain just that. They disappear amongst the rocks to report their findings to their new young leader called Tadickadee.

30

Cutnuts & Badger's Dance

The next morning Badger cooks some breakfast over the fire, and sees to it his cargo is fed. He is preparing to continue on when he sees a singular rider just over the horizon. He looks closer as the rider seems to be on a collision course. Badger has found many clever ways to conceal all of his weaponry that would give him away if it was found by the Mordagi. The only weapon visible to the naked eye is his dagger. For a few moments he considers that might have been a mistake. That thought passes quickly after he senses recognition. The lone rider gets to the halfway point when Badger makes a definite identification. He can't make up his mind to be happy or angry. I mean after all he was serious when he told everybody to head home. The rider stops short giving Badger a big grin.

"Jolo, what the hell do you think you are doing?"

"After you left some of us drew straws to see who would disobey the orders to help you. We decided that no matter what you had to have at least one of us at your side. I won the draw."

"You call this winning. I appreciate this Jolo, but I face my own destiny now."

"You mean our destiny. By the way what's with the wagon."

Finally Badger concedes he is not alone.

"What you see before you Jolo is our way into Gitch's lair. Take a look at these papers. The real owner of this freak show for lack of a better word is no longer in need of them. We are going to pass right through the gates of the city."

Badger reaches in a pocket to reveal the documents to Jolo. Jolo showing mild interest at first shows downright enthusiasm when he realizes Badger's plan.

"This is a great plan. With the real slave trader gone you have your ticket in. I guess that leaves just me to plan my way in."

"I have it Jolo. When we get close we will leave your horse in a safe place, then we will just make a cubby hole for you to stay hidden in till I get through. That should not be to difficult. Besides they are going to be looking for Badger. A single man trying to sneak his way in."

In a week's time the two will find out the outcome of this plan one way or the other.

During that week the fighting between Argonnean alliance forces, and Mordagaiian forces has become a string of holding actions on the Mordagi side. Hold, retreat, hold, retreat. The newly formed alliance has made it to the other side of the mountains in record time. As they prepare to set foot back on home soil Torman talks with Hixen.

"It has felt so great to be taking back land from the Mordagi. We will never be able to properly pay you back for everything you have done."

"Nothing personally Torman but I am just a soldier doing my job. My orders were to protect my country if violated. I am pleased it has been to your favor I will admit. As neighbors you have always respected the borders."

Grandago was a huge city. There was a thirty foot wall completely surrounding the city made from brick, and clay. There were sentry posts evenly spaced throughout the entire wall. All sentries had another post within sight, and shouting distance on both sides of them. There were a dozen gates manned around the clock by Gitch's personal guard. Coffle would hand pick men for this duty then submit his picks to Gitch for final approval. It was right around dusk when Badger approached the main city gate. He brings his conveyance to a halt when a guard orders him to stop. The compliment of men at the gate is 12 as Badger makes a mental note as he listens to his questioner.

"What is your business here?"

"Entertainment. These fools in the back are headed for Shebith's games. I have the paperwork right here."

Badger reaches into a inside pocket of his coat, and produces the paperwork. He hands it to the guard showing little interest. The guard looks at it closely. As he does three of his comrades walk over to look at the wagon. They walk around it several times then lose interest confident there is no threat. Badger is handed back the paperwork at which point he passes into the city of Grandago. After he is well away from the gate he finds a deserted alley.

In the dark Jolo appears out of a cubby hole.

"Well Badger we have made it in. Exactly where do you think she is at?"

"My first guess is the royal palace. cutnuts personal quarters. If not then the Archaic Temple."

"Makes sense. What do you propose we do with this lot in the wagon."

"As much as I hate to do it we hand them over to the gladiatorial games. If not we will give ourselves away."

Jolo just gives a nod in agreement.

"We will wait til about four in the morning to make our move. Until then let's get a few hours rest while we can."

The palace is one huge masterful art work. Columns made of marble, floors of fine granite, dozens upon dozens of rooms. The palace also has three floors with a tower on both ends. It is a very quiet morning as most of the city sleeps including the royal family. Doing some reconnaissance before resting Badger had figured where the outside guards were posted, and gotten a sense of the patrols timing also. Using a place along the wall with a small amount of foliage they use for cover the two make their way over with a grapple hook. Once over they pull the grapple hook to them so they can hide it. They find themselves in a very wide courtyard. There is a fountain in the distance. In the middle a statue of Emporer Gitch himself. Staying as close to the wall as possible they find what they beleive to be a set of wide stairs going inside. At this spot there are three guards. Using a large fragment of marble he found along the way he tosses it way past the guards. When it lands in the darkness the sound catches the guards attention. They all walk towards the sound. Two of them unsheath swords while the third brings out his crossbow. During this Badger, and Jolo creeping along in the darkness enter the open archway. Looking down the corridor it is lit by evenly spaced torches the entire length. The men are able to sidestep several patrols. As time passes Jolo reminds Badger sunrise is not far away. Badger reluctantly acknowledges.

In a passageway by a door two guards stand watch. It has been a long night, and the men know just a couple hours are left. without warning one man clutches his throat falling to the ground with a metal object sticking out. The other is quick to react as he tries to draw his sword, but finds himself pinned against the wall by two intruders. Jolo holds a knife to the guards throat. Badger quietly talks.

"where is Cutnuts living quarters?"

The guard just gives a cold stare back.

"Look here you son of a bitch you are going to tell me. I will make your last minutes agonizingly painful. Tell me what I want to know, and live."

The guard then turned his eyes.

"That way. Second floor on that end."

"Is Miranda there to?"

"You mean his wife?"

Badger delivers two strong punches into the guards abdomen. Jolo keeps him from slumping.

"You know what Jolo? I think I have what I need."

In the next instant the guard goes limp as Badger puts a dagger in his ribs.

"I thought you were going to let him live Badg."

"I lied. Let's go."

They start to leave when Jolo puts his hand on Badger's shoulder.

"Wait a minute. This is not the way he said."

"I know. Do you really think he told us the truth? We are going to do the opposite."

In just a few minutes they make their way up to the second floor by using a outside walkway. Being very quiet they find a open door guarded by three men. It is difficult to tell but Badger beleives there is a large interior with furniture. He tosses a throwing star to Jolo. They act swiftly as instantaneously they take two down with throwing stars. The third receives a crossbow shot from Jolo before he can cry out a alarm.

"Fantastic work Jolo."

The two walk to the opening. There is just a little light from a torch. From observation a couch of sorts covered with fur with a large wooden table just a few feet from it. He sees the outline of a open archway. He whispers to Jolo to keep watch while he goes inside. Jolo gives him a nod in agreement. Badger gets to the archway. He makes out the voices of two people. His heart jumps several beats as he recognizes the sound of his love. The distress so evident in her voice.

"Tonight you will submit to my will. I have finally had the chains removed. Accept your position as mine, and your life will be much more tolerable."

"There is only one man I will give myself to."

Miranda falls back against the bed as Cutnuts slaps her hard across her left cheek. She just looks back at him with bitterness. Drops of blood forming on the corner of her mouth.

"You know Miranda I don't see what you see in this Badger. If he is not dead yet he will be within a few days. It is enevitable. I will let you in on something. Your so called hero has brazenly come here to save you. All he will accomplish is his own death."

"He is here?"

"He actually led a raiding party on Ohno. From what we can tell after that he sent them all back. He will never make it past the gates into the city. You will forget him."

Cutnuts reaches down grabbing Miranda by the wrist. He forces her up against a wall. She tries to slap him but he stops her. He kisses her only to be kneed in the groin. He falters for only seconds. With his grip loosened Miranda starts to make a break. Anticipating this Cutnuts trips her. She falls hard to the floor. Reaching down Cutnuts grabs her hair.

"I was hoping not to go to the whip but you just won't be reasonable. I did not want to mark your beauty, but you leave me little choice."

He looks over to a barren place on the wall where a peg sticks out.

"Is this what you are looking for you son of a bitch?"

"who dares interfere with my . . ."

It quickly occurs to Cutnuts after he turns that Badger has indeed got past the city gates.

"My nemesis has arrived. You have been much more a problem then we ever thought possible Badger."

"Let go of her hair now."

Cutnuts looks down at Miranda, and lets go putting his open hands in front of him. Miranda fights to stay conscious as she lay in place.

"Of course. Anything for a guest of your import. What next. Fight like a man or shoot me with one of your cowardly weapons?"

At this point Jolo walks in next to Badger. Badger takes off his exposed gunbelt handing it to Jolo.

"Badger what are you doing? We don't have time for this. We have got to get her out of here. He deserves no honor."

"Maybe so Jolo but for Miranda's suffering he is going to pay. Besides he aint nothing anyway." cutnuts charges Badger upon that insult. Badger goes with the impact as they tumble over a chair. Badger gets in the first two solid hits against Cutnut's jaw. Badger begins a headlock which is shattered after receiving two elbow jabs into his ribs. Both parties separate. As they reposition the taunting continues.

"She will prove to be quite a prize once I have broken her don't you think Badger."

"It will never be more then a dream for you."

Cutnuts laughs then delivers a glancing blow to Badger. By this time both men are bleeding from cuts on their faces. The two combatants then lock hands trying to force each other back. Finally Badger gets the leverage tossing his opponent over his shoulders. Cuthuts reaches for a piece of broken chair when suddenly he feels a stream of blood from his left ear. He looks at the wall, and sees a freshly thrown star indented in the wall. He just looks up at Badger.

"Hand to hand remember."

Cutnuts starts to get up only to receive several punches. He slumps to the ground barely conscious. Badger grabs him by the shoulder blades. He drags him outside where he throws him off the second floor onto a secluded walkway making sure to snap his neck as he let's go just to leave nothing to chance. He hurries back to Miranda's side. Kneeling down to her he whispers her name. Barely conscious she answers him as he gently holds her head in his arms.

"Is it really you my love? Tell me I am not seeing an apparition of the mind."

"I am real. Many took part in this mission so I could get to you. Jolo is still with me. He is going to get you out safely. I will join you after I take care of something. Right now you need to rest."

With those words she falls into a sleep.

"What exactly do you have to take care of Badger?"

"I am going to get into the Archaic Temple of the Brethren as it is called, and find that diamond of theirs. I will destroy this menace. Remember what I said earlier."

Jolo gives a somber nod.

"I know I can depend on you my friend. Once we get outside we will go our separate paths till hopefully we rendevous like planned."

With that said Badger picks up Miranda into his arms with great care. He gingerly holds her tight to his chest. With his gunbelt put back on by Jolo they make their escape the same way they came in. Outside the palace they place Miranda in a well placed cubby hole. Badger takes out the official papers that got him past the gates.

He hands them to Jolo. They shake hands holding back words. Neither truly expecting Badger to live through this assault on the Archaic Temple. Good luck is automatically inferred anyway. As Jolo makes it back through the gates with relative ease he notes the sunrise is just minutes away. Meanwhile, Badger has found the part of the city where the Archaic Temple is at. It is somewhat secluded from everything else which doesn't surprise Badger. There are several steps leading to the front doors. He counts a half dozen men lazily guarding the entrance. The Temple appears to be two stories squared off except the front that does have a pyramidal shape. One other thing he notices is that there is a wide area of open ground maintained on all sides. From his standing position at the corner of a building he takes a look at his sidearm to make sure it is fully loaded. He checks to see how many extra magazines he has also. He allows himself one thought as he starts to take a step forward with his sidearm in his right hand.

"Better to live a short life you can be proud of then a long life with nothing to show for it."

Then he abruptly stops. He notices a figure in a dark robe making his way around a corner. Some kind of symbol on the front. Badger takes a chance. Before the newcomer can see him, and raise the alarm Badger plants a star in his forehead. He drags the body out of sight. Then he puts on the robe.

Meanwhile, guards have found Cutnut's dead. The alarm is sounded throughout the palace. Coffle hears the voices of men as they run down the passageway. He opens the door from his room halting men in their tracks.

They quickly let Coffle aware of Cutnuts death.

"What of the Emperor?"

"The Emperor is safe. He is by his son's side as we speak."

"You go find me the Captain of the guard. Tell him to report to me immediately. I will be with the Emperor understood."

"Yes.

The guard with a dozen others waste no time in following the orders.

31

Evil Vanquished

The rays of the sun have started to make their way across the forest Eld. Stretching for miles amongst the trees the camp of Argonnes, and Covehi troops stir. They prepare meals before starting back in on their pursuit of the Mordagi. Since clearing the mountains Hixen has kept his force a cohesive army. He is walking among the men when he notices Torman off by himself staring off into the woods.

"Did the big fight you told me about happen over there Torman?"

Torman is quite solemn as he answers.

"Yes. We are only a couple of miles away from that hollow ground. At the time I was not willing to admit defeat, but deep inside I wondered if I would ever see this part of my homeland again. The fight has been so hard."

"The Covehi have the deepest respect from us Torman. We shall finish pushing the Mordagi to their Emperor's door. When that happens your people will be able to have back the lives you deserve."

"Thank you Hixen. Let's eat breakfast so we can keep up the advance on set stomachs."

Hixen gives Torman a couple of pats on his shoulder as they go to replenish themselves.

Unknown to them the Mordagi have at this point made a strategic withdrawal to the Koomeron pass. The only troops not pulled back are the troops in the north at Morril, and the troops overseeing the Hykolite territory. The Koomeron pass is the door to the Mordagi homeland. There is a solid reason for that. To the north is the Koomeron depression which is three miles wide with an unknown depth that goes all the way to the shore of the Spart ocean. To the south a huge mountain range which eventually levels out to transform into part of the Okoba swamp. The pass itself is narrow at just half a mile wide. Perfect defense to force a large army to squeeze into.

The men guarding the entrance to the Archaic Temple have had a long uneventful night, and are looking forward to their releif as a visionist walks toward them. The visionist is over half way there when a approaching horse gallops into sight. The guards quickly start to look alive. The visionist throws off all pretense as the robe is flung off revealing the true identity. Badger flings a grenade right in the middle of the guards. They all die instantly from the explosion. Even the entrance doorway is set ajar from the explosive force set loose by Badger. The galloping horseman is practically on top of him as he yells in outrage at Badger. The Blackard does not get to fulfill his killing dive as Badger delivers a shotgun blast point blank in his chest. The extremely elegant blade in his hand falls to the ground as does his body. His mount shocked by the proximity of the gun blast rears up in terror. Badger continues to react quickly. He grabs the reigns of the horse, and in succession mounts the animal. Badger gallops directly through the door. It opens to a wide stairway in the middle offset by hallways on it's side. Badger hesitates for only seconds as he throws the shotgun back on his back replacing it with one of his sidearms. A Mordagi soldier runs from the left hallway to confront Badger. Still not missing a beat Badger fires one shot then prods the horse up the stairs. Behind him lay the enemy.

At the palace grounds the explosion is not unnoticed by Emperor Gitch nor his cadre of officers.

"He has made it to the Temple Coffle. Palmaroy, take Grandago's full garrison if necessary to destroy him."

"Yes Emperor."

"Coffle, see to it all Blackards within these city walls take on palace security duties immediately. I also want to see Hob."

At the second floor Badger has emptied a clip of ammunition clearing out guards from the only archway he finds up there. He dismounts noting his transportation has taken injury in it's flank from an arrow. He enters a great hall. In the middle is a red diamond glowing brilliantly. It rests on a ornately decorated stand. The only other thing in the room is a being standing next to it.

"You are quite something Badger. Every time you should die you don't. Now here you are ready to destroy our god. What arrogance you have."

"That's right Hob."

Badger fires several shots dropping Hob where he stands. Not wasting any time he walks up to the diamond. Using a small chisel, and hammer he had in a pocket he quickly makes a indention in the diamond. He takes out the last grenade he brought with him from earth. He hears Mordagaiian reinforcements coming up the stairs. He places the grenade in the niche he created. Taking a final look down at Hob he pulls the pin.

"Looks like checkmate friend."

Badger takes a huge leap towards the entrance to the room. He feels the concussion from the grenade as it goes off. The diamond shatters into a thousand pieces. The glow it gave off also gone. Badger laying on the ground shakes his head. He rolls himself over to see Mordagi troops all around him. Several with crossbows ready to shoot. Some holding sharp daggers so he could see them. To his surprise they seem unsure of themselves. Without words several start pulling back their weapons. Then as someone new enters orders are given to withdraw from the room. The order is obeyed. Badger decides to slowly get up while leaving his weapons holstered for the moment. He finds himself facing Palmaroy the highest ranking Mordagi present. Badger stands still as Palmaroy circles him slowly. After the third time he stops to face Badger face to face.

"I feel a force has been lifted from my mind Badger. I also do not think I am alone. We have brought on a destruction I have no reason to justify."

"Did your people truly lose control of yourselves to that."

Badger points to the pedestal that use to hold the diamond.

"I swear to you yes."

"Take me to Gitch. It is time for the Mordagi to stop yourselves, and do the right things."

Palmaroy listens to Badger. He nods agreement.

"Come with me Badger."

Palmaroy leads Badger solemnly back to the palace gates where Blackards stop them. Out of the three there is a conference between them. One seems to still hold the view that the war has justification, and verbally makes his intentions clear when he steps towards Badger. As Badger puts his right hand on the handle of his sidearm the other two Blackards pull there comrade in arms to the side forcefully. A Mordagi regulaR soldier is waved to the gate. Palmaroy sends him with a message to the Emperor. The wait is short. A group of about twenty arrive at the front gate. Amongst this crowd is the Emperor himself, Coffle, and a assortment of regular palace guard. As Gitch faces off with Badger the leader of the Mordagi shows a burning anger in his eyes, but he holds it in check as if to acknowledge their heinous behavior. He is the first to speak.

"They have told me you totally blew up the eye, along with Hob not to mention quite a few of our men."

"I did Gitch. The evil that festered, grew, consumed everything has been terminated. Even though it is your people have some atoning to do."

"Yes. There is much to talk about, and set right. We should go sit down inside."

"I suppose I could get some peace talks started. Lead the way."

32

Ending Of A War

Less than a week later alliance forces of the Covehi/Argonnes look ahead into the mouth of the Koomeron pass. From a patch of higher ground the figures of Hixen, Torman, Wallow, Berlox, and Glite watch intently making observations. What they see is not encouraging. Wall to wall enemy across the entire pass.

"This is going to be bloody."

"It sure is Glite. Of course when you back a animal into a corner it is always a fight."

"This is interesting. I don't know why, but there seems to be movement in the center Torman."

"Hixen, let me see your looking glass."

During this indeed a gap was made in the center of the Mordagi forces. From that gap four riders leave the line stopping at the mid point between the forces. One of them holding a flag of truce. With the distance it is hard to see facial features, but Hixen remarks to the rest one has a resemblance to Emperor Gitch himself. Torman remarks back.

"There is no way. Gitch is still in Grandago. This is some sort of trick."

Hixen still not sure what to think decides after a few minutes he has no real choice, but to send someone out there to find out what they want.

151

"Torman, how about you, Wallow, and Glite go out there to parley. See if you can figure out what they are up to."

Within minutes from the Alliance line three riders start towards the midline point from their respective side. As they get closer Torman starts to rub his eyes. Simultaneously from Torman, and Glite they make identification.

"I don't beleive it. Badger!"

"Yeah Glite, but the real question is what is he doing with Gitch?"

"Only one way to find out."

"So true."

The men close the gap.

"It is good to see you alive Badger."

"Thanks my friend. It has been a long journey. I present to you Emperor Gitch, General Livencurse Japney, and the red eyed fellow Graw. They are here to surrender."

Wallow catches himself just in time to keep from falling out of the seat as he looks at his opponent's in total shock.

Even as Torman hears the words they are slow to register.

"Did you just say surrender?"

"Yes I did Torman. The war is over. That other eye did exist."

"I'll be a son of a bitch. What have you got to say Gitch?"

"We unconditionally surrender to you. There is also much we are ashamed of beyond beleif."

"Torman, don't you think it would be a good idea to get Hixen down here to hear this to."

Torman still somewhat bewildered by the sudden turn of events acknowledges Badger's point.

"Go get him Wallow. You are a swamp chameleon are you not Graw?"

"That is true. As a participant I am here to witness the surrender. With that our agreement with the Mordagi is over."

Wallow does just that as he pulls back the reigns of his mount, and gallups back as quick as he can.

As he gallups off Badger senses Torman tensing up.

"You know something Gitch ever since you killed my family I never dreamed I would have you in front of me like this."

"You are not the only one to lose loved ones in this conflict Torman.

Badger notices Torman slowly reaching for his sword hilt. He prods his horse to step in between them. As he does so he locks eyes with his friend.

"It's over Torman. The killing has to stop now. You kill him now it is nothing less then murder. That's not you."

Badger watches as Torman's grip on the sword hilt tightens. His hand turns red as he fights the conflict inside him. Then the fight is over as he loosens then let's go.

Badger just smiles.

"Now is the time when we can regain our lives, and live anew."

Hixen rides up unable to suppress a smile.

"Badger still alive, and in the flesh. So the diamond that was projecting a evil influence was actually real."

"It sure was Hixen. I told Gitch once he surrendered to you the terms were up to you. However, we did talk amongst ourselves about a couple things."

Hixen just looks at Badger with total admiration.

"Is that so Badger."

"Gitch has promised compensation to those who lost loved ones in this war, has agreed to whatever occupation forces you wish to station on their territory, a dismissal of their army, and acceptance of alliance controlled government if it is felt necessary. Also the surrender took place the moment we left the line."

True to his word Gitch allowed a large occupation force to watch over him. The Mordagi stood down their army maintaining only a small armed civil authority to handle internal problems. One last thing that happened was a small number of cases where the evil influence was not the full reason for some acts of brutality. The influence was there, but it only intensified the bad seed certain individuals were. These few cases were handled by a tribunal of three people. The Covehi, Argonnes, and Sanders all three picked a person to be on this tribunal. The Covehi picked Badger, Argonnes picked

Hixen, and last Sanders picked Rippledutch. Out of 15 trials 9 were found innocent. The 6 guilty had death penalties carried out on them immediately. All were swift with one exception. Shebith Gitch was placed into the Gladiatorial ring to face the savage animals she had brought in. Twenty minutes was all it took for the beasts to tear her apart. It was ironic that the only game that actually took place was the one she was in. Ironic, but fitting at the same time. Before the trials though Badger had traveled back to the Sanders territory where those from his raiding party had taken up protection. They were watching over Miranda's recovery in the town of Horganpoes Ring. Resting up well her bruises were still not completely gone when Badger was finally able to rejoin her. As he rode into town the first person he recognized was Fluffy just walking out of a tavern. As he started to say something Fluffy looked up to see him.

"Badger. You pulled it off."

"It was all of us Fluffy. It could not have happened without all the sacrifices, and committment of everyone. Where exactly is Miranda at."

"She is at the Shepherd's inn just a little ways down the street. Upstairs. She is doing well. Jolo, and the rest have been seeing to that."

Badger smiles. He knew she was in good hands when Jolo took her to safety. He makes it to the doorway, and silently looks in. The door is mostly open as Miranda sits up gently in the bed looking over a piece of paper with some writing on it. He gazes on her beauty for just a moment. Finally he can bear it no more as he taps on the wood frame. She looks up. She cries out Badger's name as he moves to the bed, and sits down embracing her in the most gentlest hug possible. The embrace lasts for what seems like a eternity for the both of them. When they loosen their grip Badger wipes away tears from Miranda's cheeks.

"I will never leave you again my love. I will never break my promises I have made to you."

"Badger, my love. You have no doubts about a life with me?"

"None at all. We shall have a family that we will grow old with, and be proud of."

Miranda pulls Badger closer to her so as to passionately lock lips.

Once Miranda has gotten a few more days of rest the group rejoin the Covehi in the new town of Liberty which is being built.

Fluffy staying back in his land. As he picks back up in his Bormitian excavations he, by mere coincidence, learns of Snackle's involvement in the tavern events. Needless to say Fluffy Flambay finds no humor in this whatsoever. So Snackle, unaware of Fluffy's new found knowledge, finds himself alongside him on a very narrow trail the following day. The sun is bright, and the drop off on his right is several hundred feet. Late that day people say a solitary Fluffy returned in a rather good mood. He never lost a beat as he reported to the townspeople he was in search of a new apprentice since Snackle had accidentally fallen off his horse at the worst place possible. Within a week a new apprentice was accepted, and Snackle's early demise was never officially questioned. In the Sander's mind a war hero must have some latitude. After all, Snackle never was overly bright.

33

Beginning A New Era

"I have got to say that after all these years I still think some night I am going to wake up to find all this a dream Torman."

"You have seen alot my friend. Let's go back down where O'zar is."

Badger gives a nod of agreement. The two friends head back down the trail.

At the end of the path they enter the town of Liberty. The streets are mostly deserted as they walk to Badger's house since it is so late. When he gets there he sees O'zar patiently standing next to his horse. The animal has a stunning butterscotch colored coat to it.

"Dad. Did you have a nice walk?"

"A very soothing one son. Make me proud of how you handle the position of General. The resposibility is great."

"I will always fight for what is right. The beleifs you have passed on to me shall not leave me."

"If your mother could see you now. Tomorrow your time shall begin. I will see you at the appointed time."

"Yes father. Sleep well."

"You to. See you tomorrow also Torman."

The sun is shining brightly over the land as the council has gathered in Liberty for the momentous occasion to pass on the crown of rule to O'zar. The ceremony is to be held outside where thousands have gathered by noon. Delegates from the Argonnes, Covehi, Sanders, and even clandestinely from the Mordagi to bear witness. Inside council chambers O'zar has noticed his father's unusual lagging. He finds his pacing interrupted by Torman who walks inside.

"There he is. The soon to be President."

"Hello Torman. You see my father anywhere?"

"Your father. I figured he was already up here, and I probably just missed seeing him."

The two give each other concerned looks.

The men head to the door.

"Stay here O'zar I will grab a couple of men, and go check on your father. There is probably a simple reason for his absence."

"Nice try Torman. We can just grab men along the way."

As they make it to their horses they have already assembled Tiget, Tack, and Quist. All three men sons of well known fighters in the Mordagi fight. Outside Killamon, and Illio notice the urgency of the men.

"Torman, where are you all headed?"

"By chance Illio have either of you two seen Badger today?"

The two men exchange glances. Illio answers.

"No we haven't."

Seeing the concern on Torman's face the two quickly grab their mounts also to join the group as they ride off. At a fast gallop they make a straight line to Badger's home. As they ride up O'zar notes his father's horse in the front. O'zar has four men go to the front with him as two break off to go to the back. Tack stays with the mounts. O'zar calls out his father's name several times with no response. He gives the men a glance as he puts his hand on his sidearm which Badger had given him not to long ago. The men tense up as O'zar kicks the door in. The only sound heard is the breaking of timber. They enter to find no signs of trouble.

O'zar is the first to find his father. As the saying goes no one lives forever. Old age had caught up with Badger.

As he stands next to his bed Torman walks in.

"At least he lived a long life O'zar. Leaving here in your sleep is also the most peaceful way to move on." It is with a saddened heart O'zar accepts the position of President of the Council of Federated Villages. O'zar receives thunderous cheers from the crowds assembled outside for this most important event. He starts his five year term of office at age 25.

Two days later Badger receives a state funeral. Many fighters whom he had fought alongside with in the past are there. Representatives from the Sanders, Argonness, and even a Mordagaiian delegation attend. When the time comes O'zar with Torman next to him lead a wagon that holds Badger's body to the burial site. Alongside this wagon is Illio, Jolo, Itopoly, and opposite them their sons Tiget, Jumple, and Whylow in white ceremonial uniforms. The procession led as far as the eyes can see. Unnoticed during this procession a solitary wolf paying respects on behalf of a race watches in silence as it passes below it's position. If it had been noticed, red eyes shimmering, it was ignored.